RUNNING FOR MY LIFE

DEDICATION

To the many teenagers who are handed unfathomable challenges and who, nevertheless, find their way to freedom. And, to the counselors, parents, teachers, and friends who help them.

For me, many have helped, many have earned my
immutable gratitude—Georgine for one.

Running for My Life

By

Ann Gonzalez

WestSide Books

Published by WestSide Books
60 Industrial Road
Lodi, NJ 07644
973-458-0485
Fax: 973-458-5289

Library of Congress Control Number: 2008911812

International Standard Book Number: 978-1-934813-00-3
Cover illustration Copyright © by Michael Morganstern
Cover design by David Lemanowicz
Interior design by Paul Sikar

Printed in the United States of America
10 9 8 7 6 5 4 3 2 1

First Edition

Running for My Life

CHAPTER 1

My body knows which days I meet with my therapist even when my head tries to forget. Earlier in the day, right after Algebra, my feet started tapping, my legs bounced. I must've blanched to the color of my crew socks, because Margie said, "You've got therapy today. Don't you?"

"Shh!" I bit down on the sound, stopping it short. My shoulders climbed up toward my ears.

Margie tilted her head and gave me a quizzical look, reminding me of my stuffed rabbit, Pedro, when his head hangs to one side. She pulled a piece of paper out of her notebook, scribbled on it, shielding the words she wrote.

"What's this?" I asked when she handed me the folded sheet. Now *my* eyebrows pushed toward the bridge of my nose. I shook my head.

"Open it," Margie said.

I sighed, as deep and as loud as I could, and made a big production out of unfolding the note. It read: *We all know and we love you anyway.* Hearts and smiles danced across the bottom of the page.

Reading the words made my ears feel hot. Margie exaggerates; not everyone knows and loves me. I felt queasy-good, nevertheless. I crumpled the paper and tossed it at her. She caught it and handed it back to me.

I stuffed it in my pocket.

Certainly not all, but many of my classmates do know that I'm seeing a therapist about my mom. There's nothing I can do about it, either. It's the good-bad part of going to a small school.

Therapy is weird. There are days when I'd rather be a five-year-old running on the playground and climbing the monkey bars instead of a responsible fourteen-year-old client riding the bus to the Professional Services Building. But that's because in therapy, you can't help but remember, and just once I wish I could forget. That's what I think about as I arrive, at least ten minutes early, to the waiting room outside my therapist's office.

As I wait, I wonder about insanity. I used to think it would be interesting to be crazy. I mean really crazy. No one would expect anything from me. They'd excuse everything I did. All I'd have to do is yell at a few invisible gargoyles and everyone would back away. Then they'd leave me alone. There are days when that's all I want—to be left alone.

Crazy sounded appealing until a couple of months ago, when I visited my mom in the hospital. She nipped at a spot of air with her fingers and whispered, "Gotcha, gotcha, gotcha," over and over again. I stood around and watched her, not sure what else to do. Then she turned to me and stuck out her tongue. I would've laughed if I hadn't felt like throwing up. I just left. As I walked out she restarted her "gotcha, gotcha, gotcha" jabber.

The doctor told me she'd been given an experimental drug to help with the psychosis. *Duh, it's not working*, I'd thought. I hated that Dad brought me to see her.

"Hi, come on in." My therapist never calls me by name when I'm sitting here in the waiting room. I guess she tries to protect my privacy. I've been seeing her for a couple of months now, and it bugs me every time. I want to know that she remembers me, knows me from a week ago.

I follow her into her office. I take the same seat that I sit in each time I come to therapy. I make the same adjustments to the pillow at my back; smile the same weak smile. Everything is the same. Next she'll ask me how I'm doing.

"So, Andrea, how are you doing?"

Samantha, my therapist, has on a black skirt with a black-and-white-checkered blouse. There's a small stain in one of the white checks. She wears a silver ring—it's new—and a black pendant necklace. I notice all these things without even looking at her. I don't know how, I just do.

"Andrea? Can you look at me?" Samantha sits back in her chair, not forward like she usually does. I don't think she understands—I can't. I simply can't.

We both sit quietly. I observe the nap in the carpet; notice the heavy footprint of the client before me and the brushes and imprints left by other clients on other days.

Samantha waits.

"Okay, I get it. You don't want to talk to me." She taps a finger on the arm of her chair. "The thing is—" She leans forward, places her elbows on her thighs. "Child Protective Services, your father—the people who want you to see a counselor—want to know if therapy is beneficial to you or not."

My stomach squeezes, relaxes, then squeezes even harder. It acts like it's mad at me.

"They sent you here, thinking that the incident with your mom might be difficult for you to process on your own. They hope that I can help you to understand her illness; help you to recognize that it isn't your fault."

I close my eyes, hoping that my ears will also shut.

"You know, Andrea, that whatever you say to me is confidential, except for the few special circumstances we talked about in the first session. This means I won't talk to CPS or your father about anything we discuss in our sessions—"

An easy promise to keep since I don't plan on speaking—not now, not ever.

"—However I would like to let them know—in a general way—how things are going. Basically, I'd like to tell them whether coming here is helpful to you, and I'd like to know what you think as well, because I'm not sure." Samantha moves forward in her chair, sits at the edge.

The carpet is a blue-and-gray checkerboard. There are squares on Samantha's shirt, squares in the rug, square frames on the wall, and there are squares on the CPS forms. So many boxes clamoring to be filled in completely by black and blue pens.

"Andrea? Are you still with me?"

I guess Samantha sees things, too. She could see that I was lost in a square maze.

"I can't tell. Is coming here helpful to you?" she asks.

Samantha would probably dance a little jig if I answered her question, if I would say something, anything. I wish I could.

"If you truly are getting something out of coming here, week after week, sitting on the couch, observing the carpet, well, then I don't want to take it away from you. But—" Samantha takes a deep breath in, speaks with the exhale "—you look like a kid in trouble. I look at you and I wonder—" She turns her eyes to the carpet. I think she's trying to ease the pressure, to give me space. "—I wonder, 'What the hell did her mother do to her?'"

There's a slam. No, no, no! My breath is fast, my heart screeches. I hear yowls—an agitated cat. Where's the door? I can't see. It's dark and bright. Shit. Can't she hear me? Am I screaming? No, no, no! No! Shit. Everything's a shadow. I can't see. I'm in a darkened room in the bright of day.

Samantha slides her foot onto "my" square of the rug, drawing my attention.

"—Okay, Andrea, take a couple of deep breaths. In, one, two, three; out, one, two, three." Samantha breathes in and out to help me regulate my breath. She gives me something to imitate.

We breathe in and out, together, for several minutes.

I sweat. I shake. Thankfully, my blindness dissolves. Slowly, the blue of the couch, the carpet, the painted glass egg that sits on the side table, Samantha's black pendant and her warm brown eyes all come into focus. I close and open my eyes again; tears soften the edges.

"How about this?" Samantha pulls her foot back to her chair; my eyes follow. "I see that this is difficult for you to talk about—" She places a hand on each knee. "So, how about if I talk to your principal, Dr. Miller, and find out how your studies are going?"

I wait, listen.

"I won't talk about you or what's happening here." Samantha leans forward. "If everything is okay at school, I think we can assume that therapy is helping, and we'll continue as we are."

I take a breath, wait.

Samantha lifts her right hand, extends it to me. "If not, you and I will discuss your options. Okay?" She moves her fingers back and forth, drawing a line to connect us.

I feel pressed against the couch; the room feels small. Samantha is so close. I nod my head. That I can do.

"Good. That's good," she replies.

I nod my head a few more times.

"We'll talk about this in Thursday's session, okay?" Samantha asks.

I nod again. This is the most that I've "said" to Samantha since I first started seeing her.

Samantha sits back in her chair. I do, too.

When I stand to leave, I drop my bag, accidentally on purpose, if there is such a thing. Bending down to pick it up, I touch the carpet; I press my hand into it. It feels soft like rabbit fur, like Pedro. I wish I could lie down and roll myself up in it, pick it up and wear it like a cape. Now that's nutty. I hope my handprint is still here on Thursday. I'd like to have it wave at me for an entire session.

As I leave the office, I touch my hand, remembering soft, remembering carpet, remembering the brush of fur. Passing through the waiting room, the next client gives me a thin-line smile. I sling my bag over my shoulder and force my hands into my pants pockets. What if that person, that lone person sitting in the beige chair, saw me rubbing my hands and thought I was crazy?

I move so fast, I don't even look at the shoes whose soles will next be imprinted in Samantha's carpet. Hurrying through the front door, I'm certain that crazy is the last thing I ever want to be.

CHAPTER 2

It is a relief to step outside. My heart still races. I want to walk down the pathway, down the street, down the highway; I want to walk and walk and walk. I wonder if I kept on going, without stopping, what would give out first? Would exhaustion make me drop to the ground in a deep sleep, or would blisters and muscle cramps anchor my feet to the asphalt? Is it possible to be so tired, for your body to hurt so much, that you can't take another step? I can imagine being that tired, hurting that much.

Dad toots the horn of his hundred-year-old navy blue Datsun. Idling at the end of the walk, it sputters the nose-crinkling exhaust of an old, well-loved automobile. He washes and polishes his car at least once a week and is lightning fast when it comes to cleaning off bugs and other splat. He's a goof about his funny old car.

Dad reaches over from the driver's seat and opens the passenger door.

"Hey, kiddo." Dad is always cheerful. Even when everything is going wrong—Mom is coming apart, there are problems at his job—he'll still be all, "Hey, kiddo." Sometimes he makes me mad with his chirpy banter.

I put on my seatbelt, look out the passenger window, and we drive away. One of the things I love about my dad is that he's okay with silence. Even though I'm not looking at him, I can see him tap his fingers on the steering wheel and check the rearview mirror. It's like he's content even when nothing is happening.

"Are you working tonight?" I ask. I can talk to my dad and to Margie and to most people. Samantha's office is the only place I can't find my voice.

"Yep. I'll be going in at ten o'clock. Will you be okay?"

"Dad. You ask me that every time you work at night. And that's a lot of times."

"Well, you know how to reach me, just call—"

" - 9 - 1 - 1!" We both say it at the same time, laughing. Dad became a 911 operator years ago; we joke about calling 911, but it isn't really funny.

I have no idea what I'm going to "be" or "do" when I'm older. Whatever it is, I hope I like my work as much as my dad likes answering emergency phone calls. He was a police officer before he became an emergency operator. I think he gave it up because he didn't like carrying a gun.

"Margie's coming over. We're going to study for our psych test on Friday," I tell him.

"Oh, that's good. I'm glad you'll have company. Shall I order pizza or something?" Dad asks.

"Sure."

I stare back out the window. Everything rushes by at breakneck speed. Dark is dropping onto the town like a blanket. It reminds me of therapy, and I want to claw my way out from under the thickening dusk.

"Dad?"

I can feel him turn his head toward me.

"Is Mom coming back?" I ask, without looking at him.

He takes a deep breath in. Maybe he prefers silence to conversations like this. Who wouldn't? "I don't know, kiddo. I really don't know." He grips the wheel; his fingers have lost their dance.

"She might then?"

"Maybe." He scratches the back of his neck. "First we want to be sure she isn't a danger to herself or anyone else."

The trees hurtle by—I'm flying through space and I'm only traveling a short distance. Time races us through the streets.

"Do you want her to come home?" Dad asks.

"Sometimes I do." My head turns away from the window. For a brief moment, Dad and I make eye contact— then we both look away.

"And—" I shift in my seat. The heater in the stupid Datsun must be out of whack; it's a thousand degrees in the car. I open the window. Speaking into the blurring trees and clamoring wind, I add, "— sometimes I don't."

Dad reaches over and puts his hand on mine. I realize I've been wrenching the car seat, gripping it and twisting. When Dad covers my hand I relax a little. He slows down; the trees stop rushing. I don't pull away from Dad. We stay just as we are for a moment or two.

Dad's palm is radiating heat. His fingers are surprisingly soft—not calloused and rough, the way you'd expect from a man who works on his car and around the house. I want to let him know that I appreciate this gesture, that I appreciate him. But I can't.

"Is that bad, that I'm not sure?" I'm leaning out the window like a dog hungry for air.

"No. No, kiddo. It isn't bad at all. I'm not sure either." Dad lets go of my hand, runs his fingers through the few hairs left on his head, and then seizes the steering wheel like he wants to rip it out of the dashboard.

"Andrea—what your mother did—" Dad hits the dash with the flat of his hand. This surprises me; I flinch. "—it wasn't your fault." Dad looks like he's scanning the road for words, his head bobs left and right.

"You're a great kid," he says. "That's what I'm trying to tell you—you are the *best*." He leans back into his seat, blankets my hand again, and turns onto our street. He lets go of a long breath of air.

"I think we both want Mom to be well again, the way she used to be. Then it would be great to have her home again." Dad sneaks a peek at me then moves in toward the steering wheel, holding it close in both arms.

Pulling into the driveway, with his face lit from the side by the porch light, Dad looks as old as his car.

CHAPTER 3

"Okay, who are you going to be dating come prom time?" Margie, like my dad, is also perpetually upbeat. How is it that I am forever surrounded by cheerful people?

"Uh, Margie, we're freshmen?" I raise my eyebrows and point my chin at her in my best "get-a-clue" posture. "Freshmen!"

I flip my notebook sideways so I can read the notes I scribbled along the edge of the page. "Last I heard, proms were for juniors and seniors."

"Always be prepared. Isn't that the Boy Scout motto or something?" Margie replies.

"Maybe, but in case you haven't noticed, we aren't boys. See, that's the funny thing about Boy Scouts. They're mostly boys!" I say, as I toss my stuffed bunny, Pedro, at Margie. I'm sitting at the top of my bed; she's lying across the foot. She catches Pedro.

"Oh, I love Pedro," she says, completely ignoring my sarcasm. She grooms his ears and fluffs his tail. "If I don't get asked to the prom when we are juniors, I'm taking him." Margie waggles Pedro at me, then rolls onto her back, letting my floppy stuffed rabbit sit on her chest.

"You do that. I'll go with a Teletubby and we'll both be locked up for being lunatics." The inevitable silence follows. It's always there—that pause or beat—that everyone takes after I make a "crazy" joke.

"I thought the Teletubbies were gay." Now she's bouncing Pedro by pulling on his ears.

"The Teletubbies are aliens with TVs in their stomachs! How can they be gay?" I grab Pedro from Margie's frenzied puppeteering. "Can we get back to psychology? Please?"

"Oh, all right." Margie rolls back over and flips a couple of pages in the psychology text. "But talking about the prom is much more fun than reading about a crazy guy like Skinner. It says here that he raised his daughter in a box."

"It does not. Where does it say that?" I scoot down to the bottom of the bed so I can see what Margie is referring to. "It says he built a box for his daughter to sleep in. Not that he raised his daughter in a box," I declare, reading over her shoulder.

"Point is he kept his daughter in a box. Look, here's a picture of her." We both stare at the cute little girl, naked on top, hand pressed to the glass in front of her. I wonder if anyone can hear her when she cries.

Margie flips the page. "Ooh, looking at that gave me the creeps. Can you imagine? She was in this little box and the windows didn't open." Margie raises her shoulders and shudders.

"Hey, are you okay?" Margie asks.

She sits up and puts her hand on my shoulder. She brushes back the hair hanging over my face. I press my head between my knees; I'm rocking and embracing my legs with both arms. I am as tight and as small as I can be.

I want to let go, to answer her, but I can't. Something is happening to me, I feel sick to my stomach. I can't speak. I just rock and rock and rock.

"I'm going to get your dad." Margie grabs Pedro and puts him at my feet. "I'll be right back." Margie has been running to get help for me ever since Mom's first breakdown. In a few seconds she returns with Dad.

Even in this state, I can see him without looking at him—his face is pale, ghostly.

"Hey, kiddo, you okay?" Dad uses his soothing 911 voice. He sits next to me on the bed and gathers me onto his chest; I can't help but unravel.

"We were just reading about Skinner and his stupid box," Margie says. Her voice is high and tight.

I'm not really sure what I'm crying about, but once I start, crying is all I can do.

"That's good," Dad says. "Let it out." He sounds like he's teary-eyed too.

"Come here, Margie," he adds, "let's have a group cry." I didn't realize Margie was wet-eyed too. Usually I notice things like that.

Margie picks up Pedro, sits on the bed behind me, and we become a big clump of damp.

I know this won't last forever. Dad will have to go to work soon, our muscles will cramp and our tears will run dry.

But for right now, as the three of us—well, four including Pedro—huddle together sobbing and rocking, I'm almost happy. This is as happy as I've been in a very long time.

CHAPTER 4

"Hey!" Margie pops up behind me. She appears out of nowhere. I snuck out of the library a few minutes early. Apparently she did the same with gym.

"Did you bring him?" Last night, Margie told me to bring Pedro to school today—for her. She reaches into my locker, and picks him up by one ear. His fluffy body hangs from his cocked head.

"Come on now, be nice to him." I snatch Pedro from the air and brush his ears back so they lay flat on his head. "Have you ever noticed how round a rabbit's head is when you flatten its ears?" I hold Pedro up for Margie to see.

"*You* be nice to him. After all he's going to be my prom date." Margie pushes my shoulder. We both laugh. It feels good to be back to normal. "And since we're speaking of proms—"

"*We* aren't speaking of proms. *You* are."

"As I said, speaking of proms, I've decided I'm going to go to the prom with Matthew Davidson." Margie tugs Pedro out of my hand and sets him on top of the stack of books in my locker.

"Good, Pedro," she says, patting his head. "Behave yourself." She wags her finger at wide-eyed Pedro as she closes the locker door.

"Matthew Davidson? He's a senior this year. He won't even be here when you're a junior."

"Precisely why we need to sign up for track now. I need to get to know Matthew if I'm going to go to his prom." Steering me away from the locker and down the hall, Margie says, "Come on, we've got to get to Mr. Higgins before next period starts. Let's sprint."

"Track? Are you out of your mind?" I stop short; Margie bumps into me when I do. She seems to wince at my question. "That's crazy."

It reminds me of the game we used to play, *Mother, May I*. I abruptly turn to face Margie and she solidifies, becomes a statue. There is a pause, we are both perfectly still, then we each take a deep breath in and resume breathing on the exhale. It's the strangest thing.

When Margie comes alive, her voice is hard like a rock. "No, Andrea, I'm not crazy, loco, or mad."

She squints at me, scrunches her mouth. "It's my plan, a perfect plan. Matthew is on the track team and so is Sean." She crosses her arms. "You like Sean, so this plan has a payoff for you, too."

"Tell me what we're doing again?" I ask her.

"It's simple." Margie nods her squinty, pursed lips at me. "We're going to go out for the track team—get to know Matthew and Sean, develop our college portfolios, and get some exercise. It's such a good idea I'm amazed I didn't think of it sooner." Margie relaxes her arms, her face, and brings both palms up in a "there you have it" pose.

"This is a dumb idea on so many levels. The first being, we don't RUN!" I didn't mean to raise my voice, but track? For real? Sometimes I wonder about Margie.

"Yeah, what else?" she asks.

"Let's see." I tilt my head; tap my finger on my lips. "Hmm, what else? Oh yeah, how about the fact that we don't RUN! Last I checked, track was geared toward runners."

"Everyone knows how to run. You know how to run; I've seen you. Plus, I talked to Mrs. Cameron and she said it would really help our college profiles." As she says "profiles," Margie makes the quote symbol with her fingers.

Margie hates everything that improves her chances of getting into college. She's afraid that she's not smart enough, and that if she does get in, she'll flunk out and her mother will never be able to get over the "shame" of it all. Margie is, of course, smart, and she'll probably get into the best Ivy League school and be in the top of her class. That is, unless she continues to reject every activity that improves her high school transcript.

I've got to give it to her, though; she knows me. If there's anything that will get me to run track, college is it. Even though I absolutely, one-hundred-percent, don't want to go out for track, I'll consider anything that will improve my chances of getting into a good college and of getting scholarships. Part of me wants to run from the idea of running, but instead I stay. I stay and argue.

"Isn't it too late? Don't you have to sign up for track in September or something?" My voice is a high-pitched screech.

"Nope. Mrs. Cameron says they welcome students into track all year. Something about wanting to encourage physical fitness." Margie seems to be enjoying this.

"You mean they don't care whether you know how to run or not? What if I only had one leg? Would they still accept me on the team?" I wake up to the fact that I've been walking down the hallway with Margie. "Hey, where are you taking me?" My next class is Algebra and it's back the other way.

"To sign up for track. Like I said." Margie pushes me forward, as I press my back into her hand. "Go. Go. Just a little farther." She urges me on.

"I'll make a great runner, if the object is to go backward as quickly as possible."

"Tsk. Tsk. The first rule of sports—be positive!" says Margie.

"What has gotten into you? Be positive; be prepared. You're just a cliché-maker. Can't you say anything original?" I apply more pressure, hoping to get us moving in reverse.

Margie stops pushing me. I take an awkward step backward. I was using her push to support me and, suddenly, my brace disappeared. "Hey!" I yell, as I scramble to regain my footing. I shouldn't have called Margie unoriginal; I know better. She already thinks of herself as dull; boring; drawn, meticulously, between the lines. It's a sore spot.

"That, Andrea, wasn't nice." Margie takes a step away, then turns to face me. "Forget it. You don't have to sign up for track. It doesn't matter. I just thought it would be fun."

I look at the ceiling, certain I'll see dark clouds forming. Margie walks down the last of the hall and turns the corner. She doesn't look back, doesn't wave, doesn't offer the Margie smile. She simply disappears.

"Margie, wait up. I'm sorry." I call after her but don't take a step in any direction. I can't. My feet are glued to the tile floor. I turn this way, then that. I don't think I'll ever be able to move from this spot. Students will come and go, year after year, and they'll all ask about the girl in the hallway. *What's up with her?* they'll wonder.

I'll yell Margie's name, but she won't hear me. I'll be stuck here, unable to move, frozen in a perpetual game of *Mother, May I.* Eventually, I suppose, I'll be too tired to stand. I'll jerk and jolt and collapse in a heap of exhaustion, like a car on its last legs.

I wake from my fantasy nightmare when the bell blares the end of this period. Classroom doors open and, like Pavlov's dogs, students stream out into the hallway. I, at last, begin to move. Bang, I turn, and bump right into Sean Taylor. *The* Sean Taylor.

"Hi, Andrea." Sean—lean, tall Sean—nods at me.

I blush; at least I think I do. I'm boiling hot. But I don't have time for this. "Uh, where's the track sign-up place?" No easy banter, just right to the point.

"Mr. Higgins's class?" Sean's jeans are low on his hips, he's wearing a navy t-shirt, with a pink unbuttoned oxford over it—everything about him is relaxed.

"Yeah. Is that where you sign up?" I'm short, high strung, and as far from Sean on the cool meter as a person can be.

"Yeah. He's the coach. His room is 23A. You know, around the corner, down the stairs. Second door on the right." With his long arms and legs, Sean looks more like a basketball player than a track athlete.

"Thanks. Thanks for your help." My mouth is dry; I lick my lips and swallow my tongue. I have to find Margie. "I've gotta go," I say as I hurry down the hall.

"Hey, Andrea," Sean calls after me.

"Yeah?" I turn.

"We should go running together." Sean stands a good six inches above all the other students in the hallway. He stands out.

"I'm not much of a runner, but okay. Sure." Margie's not only creative, she's brilliant, too. "I've got to go." I turn away, then back again, "Thanks." I wave and move as quickly as I can around the corner and down the stairs to Mr. Higgins's room.

Right now, I feel like I can run as fast as Superman. I imagine that there is a flurry of papers and a little starburst in the spot where I used to be standing. Run, run, run—that's all I want to do.

CHAPTER 5

Please be there. Please.

I'm not sure whether I'm imagining things or not, but through the swarm of students I hear Margie's voice. My heart stops racing—it returns to its regular hip-hop beat.

"Thank you, Mr. Higgins. I'll fill these out and get them back to you." Margie leaves the classroom holding a curl of papers. She brings them up to her forehead and gives Mr. H a paper-salute.

"Margie, wait," I call to her, trying to be heard above the bang and clang of lockers opening and closing.

Margie takes a couple of steps toward me, then leans her back against the tile and bends one leg, pressing her heel against the wall. I can't tell if she heard me or not.

"Margie!" I call again. Hallways remind me of riverbeds in a storm—the bell rings, the hallway fills to overflowing, and then, almost as quickly, the floodwaters drop and the students disappear into their next classes.

"I'm sorry. Really sorry." I'm breathless as I approach, even though I've only been walking fast. "I didn't mean what I said."

Margie stares at me with her green eyes. Quickly, I join her leaning against the wall—it's a relief to escape her direct gaze. She hands me a piece of paper. "Here," she says.

I take the sheet, the *Hayworth High School Track Team Application Form*, from Margie. "Yep. Okay." I nod my head a few times. "You're a genius, you know. Your plan is already working."

Margie shifts so she's facing me again. "It's working? What? Tell me." She swats me with the paper she's still holding in her hand, her application I assume. I want to jump and hug her and do a little dance—Margie slapped me with a piece of paper! She forgives me.

"Well, you have to promise me that you'll teach me how to run before we actually join the team." I mime running, then tripping and falling forward.

"Very funny, McKane." Margie hits me, again, with the paper. "I'm serious, tell me."

"Sean asked me to go running with him."

Margie's jaw drops, her eyes widen. "Holy smokes; that's great!" Again she hits me with the roll in her hand. I rub my arm as though she hurt me. "We are *so* joining the team."

"I know, I know. You were right. So right." I grab Margie's arm. "But I don't know how to run. Really. I'm not sure I can run twenty-five feet, never mind a quarter mile, a mile, or whatever it is that those speed freaks run."

"Ah, I wouldn't call them speed freaks—we don't want anyone thinking the Hayworth High Track Team is full of druggies. Especially if we're on the team." Margie starts to walk down the hall and signals me to follow her by jerking her head a couple of times. "C'mon, McKane, we're just going to have to start training, that's all."

"I'm right behind you. But running to catch up." I reply.

"Do you want to go running right now? I've got shorts in my locker; I'm wearing sneakers—" she begins.

"Running shoes," I correct her.

"Right, running shoes. And yes, we need to get you in shape if you are to have any chance of keeping up with Sean," Margie replies.

I can see Margie's mind planning our training schedule, the sit-ups she'll have me do, the raw egg shakes she'll have me drink, and the weights she'll have me lift. She'll be like some *Rocky* trainer, whipping me into shape for the grand fight, run, or whatever.

"Are you ready?" Margie asks.

"Well—" I'm afraid to say yes. What if I can't run? What if I am no faster than a turtle and unable to complete a single lap? What if I let everyone down? "— I guess." I shrug my shoulders.

"We'll work on your attitude later. First, let's just get out onto the track." Margie starts to walk again, this time with purpose and determination in each and every step.

"Wait." It is my turn to stop her. "Let's get Pedro. He can be our mascot."

"Good idea." Margie nods her head. "Now you're thinking. You're getting your head in the game."

When Margie says nice things to me, which is most of the time, I feel good. Excited bubbles rise in my chest when she declares she likes my idea.

I don't tell her that my head isn't any more in the game now than it was a few minutes ago. I thought of Pedro because, for some reason, I started to worry about him. My chest tightened when I thought about him sitting on my stack of books in the dark, cramped locker.

I don't want Margie to think I am crazy for worrying about Pedro, so I don't tell her. I'll be happier, though, when he's out of the locker, back home and sitting at the head of my bed. Or better yet, timing our sprints and helping Margie and me get in shape.

As long as Margie is my friend and forgives me for my bonehead comments, I think I can do anything—even learn to run.

Chapter 6

"First—stretching is very important." Margie bends over and places her palms flat on the ground between her feet, then places her head along her left leg, then right. I can just touch my fingertips to the sandpapery surface of the track. My muscles are tight and stiff.

"How do you know this stuff?" The trees lean to the left, then right as I watch them, upside down, from between my legs. The world is like liquid when viewed from the ground.

"Now lunges." Margie moves into a deep knee bend with an outstretched leg. I groan but follow right along. "From watching the track team practice."

"Really?" I stop, roll onto the ground into a sitting position. "When did you watch practice? Where was I?"

Margie rises from her crouch and goes over to the bench at the edge of the track. She picks up Pedro. He's been watching us with his unblinking beaded eyes. "How are we doing, Pedro? Are we warmed up enough?" Margie shakes Pedro so his ears flop up and down in the affirmative.

"Margie?" I take a couple of steps toward the bench. "Really, you've been working on this scheme for awhile?" How could she have been observing track team practices and planning to join, without my knowing about it? We tell each other everything.

Margie sits with Pedro on her lap, so the two of them are watching me. "You were kind of out of it when school started." Margie pulls Pedro close, the way I do when I feel scared. "I understood. Your mom was in the hospital." She holds Pedro as close as she can; he's squished. "I needed something to do."

I turn around to look out across the football field. I breathe in the grass, the pine, the white-blue sky. "I wish you'd said something." I never considered how my mom's sickness might be hard on Margie.

"You're not mad, are you?" Margie comes to stand by me; she nudges my shoulder with hers.

"No. I'm not mad." And I'm not. I am sad, though. I wish I could leave that whole mess behind, get far away from it. I pump my legs up and down. Now, I feel ready to run. "Did you hatch any other ideas I need to know about?" I hop a few times and shake my hands. I've watched sprinters do this before they take their marks—it feels good. "Are we joining the chess club, debate team, anything else?"

"Nope, just track." Margie scurries back to set Pedro on the bench. "Warmed up?"

"Yep." I shrug my shoulders because I'm not sure how we start. Margie laughs.

"Then let's go." Margie begins by taking a few jogs in place then heads out onto the track. We run.

At first, I'm like a cold engine, chugging at the turn of the key. I'm glad no one from the track team is here to see me huffing through these first twenty feet.

After a few minutes I find my stride. I feel taller and stronger; it's weird. I run, *shh, shh, shh*. Shoulders back, chin up, *shh, shh, shh*, I continue to run. My legs are pistons, exploding downward, *shh, shh, shh. Shh, shh, shh.* It's so peaceful, *shh, shh, shh*. Even though I'm getting tired and my legs are begging me to stop, I just want to go, go, go.

We run—one lap, then two.

Shh, shh, shh. My body may punish me tomorrow, but right now I feel great.

"Hey, Margie," I manage to speak through my pounding breath.

"Yeah?" Margie matches my stride, even though I suspect she's a much faster runner than I am.

"A few weeks ago, my mom sent me this letter—" I haven't been able to tell anyone about this, but on the track, running at a steady clip, there are things I want to say. "—from the hospital."

Margie steps, steps, steps, and waits for me to say more.

"It was bad," I add.

One stride, two strides, three strides, *shh, shh, shh,* she keeps pace.

"I don't think my mom—" *stride, stride, stride,* "—I don't think she likes me very much."

"What?" Margie switches her head back and forth as she looks at me and keeps her eyes on the track ahead.

"The letter—" *shh, shh, shh,* "—it was gross." The truth is I couldn't read the whole thing, it made me sick. I stuffed it into the bottom of my locker, under a mess of papers, hoping to forget it. No such luck.

"She's sick, Andrea. That's what makes her mean." Now Margie watches me more than the track.

"Maybe." My legs churn, and I move ahead of Margie.

I hear the *thwap, thwap, thwap* and the *huh, huh, huh* of Margie as she catches up. "She loves you, Andrea. She's just sick."

"Yeah. I know she loved me—before." I surge ahead again. "I'm not so sure about now," I say through bursts of breath that Margie probably can't hear since she's behind me.

"Wait." Margie reaches out as though she's handing me a baton and touches my arm. "Pedro signaled for us to stop after this lap." She gently pulls me toward the bench that is just ahead. We both shorten our strides. We arrive at our starting point, now our finish line, bent over, breathing hard.

"Wow. I feel like puking," I say to my shoe tops, through gasps of air.

"It's kind of gross, but if you spit you'll feel better."

I peek at Margie through the strands of brown hair that are hanging over my face. She never ceases to amaze me with the things she knows.

"Running frees up junk and you don't want to swallow it back down. You want to get rid of it." Margie demonstrates by going to the edge of the grass and spitting. She spits and stands beaming an exaggerated smile. "That feels soooo good," she says.

"Okay, okay." I go to the edge and spit too. It does feel good.

"Let's rest for a minute." Margie heads to the bench. She picks up Pedro and sets him on my lap as I sit down next to her. "I don't get 'mental illness,'" she says, quoting the words with her fingers. "Is it like a virus? When will your mom get better?"

The clouds are moving fast across the sky. They swirl into shapes then explode and swirl and explode. I shiver. "I don't know. She may never get over it." I rub Pedro's nose against mine. "Schizophrenics don't, usually."

I lean over my knees, creating a dark cave for Pedro; I hug him close. "It's hereditary too." I spit onto the ground between my feet. I still want to puke.

There is the pause, the beat, the moment when Margie and I stop for just one breath.

"You are not crazy." Margie pushes my shoulder back so that we are eye to eye when she speaks. "You're not," she says again.

"Yeah—" I look down at Pedro, at his never-closing eyes. He's like me—he sees everything. "My mother wasn't crazy either. Until she was." My stomach rolls over.

"I don't care. You aren't sick and you aren't going to be." Margie reaches over and pets Pedro a few times. "Tell her, Pedro! Tell her she's the sanest person we know." She tilts the face of my sweet stuffed rabbit up so he's looking me right in the eyes. "Tell her." She waggles his head back and forth.

I brush his ears down flat. "Okay, okay."

The clouds turn gray, the sky sinister. "We'd better go. Those clouds are getting mean." I stand up. My legs lift and drop, eager to run to the building, to safety.

Margie rises, slower than I did. "Hey, thanks for running with me." She puts her arm on my shoulder and for a moment we stand and watch the pines brush against the cumulating clouds.

"Thank *you*." I bounce a couple of more times watching the darkening sky. "I like it."

"Now if I can just get Matthew to notice me like Sean's noticed you."

The woods smell damp as it prepares for rain. "He's a fool if he doesn't ask you out; if he doesn't love you." I waggle Pedro in her face. "Tell her!"

Margie laughs. She snatches Pedro from my hands. "Okay. Okay. Speaking as your personal trainer—you did great today. You're off to a great start."

I bend my knees and get in a starter's crouch, then launch myself as though a gun's gone off. It's the greatest feeling. One minute I'm small and tight, and the next I'm running; running with arms outstretched, running free.

CHAPTER 7

"Hi, come in." Thursday's session begins. "So, Andrea, how are you doing?" Samantha asks after we've hit our marks, taken our seats.

My handprint is gone from the carpet. It looks like someone vacuumed last night. Darn.

"I talked to Dr. Miller. She said that you're back on course after going through a rough period. Your grades are good, your attendance is perfect, and your attitude has improved a great deal. She said you are becoming a 'star' at Hayworth." Samantha is leaning forward, fingertips together, elbows on her knees. "I'll tell your father and CPS that continued therapy is the desired course of action. If you agree."

I nod my head.

"Thanks," I say in a whisper I barely hear myself.

I can see Samantha's eyes widen a little, her eyebrows raise the teensiest bit, her lips tug into a smile that's so small it looks like a twitch. I guess she's happy that I spoke, but doesn't want to scare me by jumping up and dancing that jig.

"You're welcome. I'm glad you're doing well in school." Samantha shifts in her seat. This is not a good sign. Scary news usually follows a change of position.

"Andrea, can you look at me?" And queasy news follows eye contact. Shit.

I look up and right back down. Samantha's eyes were soft, sensitive, caring. I couldn't stand it. Whatever she wants to tell me, she's going to have to tell me while I'm watching my square of carpet.

"You're scheduled to visit your mother again in a few weeks." Samantha waits, one, two, three. I wait, too. We breathe in unison.

"I want to support you through that visit. I'm not sure how to do that, though, without some indication from you." She waits.

I think she wants me to say something. I wish I could. My tongue feels like a bag of sand. My throat hurts, my ears hurt. I swallow and swallow.

"Do I have to see her?" My stomach is flipping around again.

"It's part of the agreement. Would you rather not?" Samantha is leaning far forward. It's like she wants to make it so that I can speak as softly as I need to and she'll still hear me.

I shrug my shoulders. I'm going to cry and I don't know why. I clutch my stomach. I must look green or something because Samantha gets up and grabs a waste can. She puts it near my foot.

"Keep breathing," Samantha says. "Keep breathing."

I inhale, one, two, three and exhale, one, two, three. Samantha is breathing in rhythm with me.

"Can you tell me what scares you about seeing her?" she asks.

I shake my head, "No." That's the truth. I can't tell her. Fear erases all my words.

Samantha raises her hands, palms up, as though she's cradling air. "Would you like to schedule a session for right after the visit?"

I vigorously nod my head in agreement.

"You know that she won't be able to hurt you, right? There will be nurses and doctors on duty. I want you to know that you'll be safe." Samantha mirrors my silent yes; her head goes up and down.

I continue to signal yes, but I wonder if Samantha understands what "safe" means. My mother doesn't have to have a knife in her hand to be dangerous.

Samantha gets up and goes into her office closet. She brings out a wooden box the size of a shoe. "I want you to take this box and put some things in it that represent safe people, places, or memories." She holds it out for me to take.

It is small, pine, simple. I open it, and there is a medallion inside. I pick up the piece of flattened metal—on it is imprinted a single word—*Freedom*. I hold the medallion up for Samantha, thinking that she didn't know it was inside.

"That's for you," she says.

I take my hand down; the medal feels heavy. "Why?" I pass my thumb over the word.

"To remind you that I know how hard you are working to free yourself." Samantha is serious, but with a small smile.

I place the token back in the box, touching the felt that lines the bottom—red felt. I've never been given anything like this before, so I'm not sure what to do or say. I have that uneasy feeling again. I wish nice people didn't make me feel sick.

"Thanks," I say.

"You're very welcome." Her eyes begin to smile, too.

With that, the tension in my shoulders lessens. Samantha looks softer, too.

"Dr. Miller mentioned that you signed up for the track team. Do you want to talk about that? Can you?"

"Maybe," I say. Then, surprising myself and, I'm sure, Samantha, I start to speak. I speak a whole sentence, one packed with words. I say, "It's probably a dumb idea—the track team—but Margie says it will look good on our college applications."

"Do you think it's a dumb idea?"

"No." Words are rising in my throat. "Really, it's a good idea."

"What makes it good?" Samantha asks.

"Margie and I have gone running a few times. She's

showing me." Speaking makes me tense—my shoulders lift, my leg bounces. "I like moving."

"How do you feel when you run?" Samantha asks.

"I, it, I feel weird—loose. I feel, I don't know, *free*, I guess." I look up at Samantha. She's watching me closely. I look away.

"Sounds nice," she says.

"Yeah, it's a nice feeling, the *shh, shh, shh* rhythm of running. Sometimes I don't want to stop. I'm not good at it or anything, I just like it." What has gotten into me? I'm talking. Talking like a chatterbox, whatever that is; talking like something that won't stop.

"It's obvious that you like it—you brighten when you speak about it." Samantha grins, chuckles, and I don't feel sick. The room seems large and open. Everything is strange.

"There's a boy, too." Now, I know I'm losing it.

"Tell me about him."

Just like that the silence comes back. The walls move in and surround me; they choke me. I drop my eyes to a footprint in the rug; it has a heavy heel. "I can't," I mutter. "Sorry."

"Nothing to be sorry about. Thank you for telling me about running."

Samantha continues to talk. I don't say another word. *Shh, shh, shh*, I listen to the rhythm of running. *Shh, shh, shh*, it's the only sound I hear.

CHAPTER 8

I prop Pedro up on a bleacher seat. That's his new, preferred, spot from which to monitor Margie and me as we practice for practice. Margie and I have been running all over the place, literally, getting ready for next week when we start training with the team.

Margie is sitting on a bench and watching the woods. I can't see her face, but her shoulders are up and she looks tense. "Hey, Margie," I try to get her attention, "Pedro says, 'Don't forget to stretch!'"

Margie keeps staring.

"Margie?"

"Yeah, yeah. I'm coming." Margie gets up, stands next to me. Her silence is a heavy weight; too much for me to lift. She's the one who talks and talks, I'm the one who stands around in the dark. I remind myself it's okay for Margie to be quiet. Once in awhile.

I finish tying my running shoes, and pull my ankle up toward my butt, trying to loosen my thigh muscles. "You know, I like running so much I don't care that I'm not fast."

"Huh?" Margie reacts as though she's surprised I said

anything. "Oh, you'll get faster." Obviously she heard me. "You're like a cat when you run—smooth."

My face prickles when Margie says that; I wonder if I'm turning red. I bend forward pretending to touch my toes—really I'm just hiding. Even though it's the bazillionth compliment from Margie, still, it makes me want to disappear.

"How many laps do you want to run?" I tug on my other foot, stretch my other thigh.

"Let's run the Old River Trail," Margie says, looking across the tracks toward the woods. "I want to do some cross country; get away from the school."

Old River Trail is a nice wind through the woods. It starts on the other side of the field, takes you through a pine forest, down by the river, near the train tracks, and loops back up to the high school. It's beautiful. Why, then, does my stomach turn in on itself?

"Really? You want to run through the woods?" I bend over again; try to manage the protests nipping in my throat. "Away from the school?" The idea of leaving the track causes my stomach to somersault. Branches have a way of closing off the sky and shutting out the light. I prefer an open field.

"Yeah, McKane, that's what I said." Margie stretches too, twists from side to side, and continues to stare off into the green and black. Even though we stand side by side, we are miles apart.

"Are you okay? You're acting weird!"

Margie takes a few steps forward toward the woods. Her back blocks my view. "I am not being weird! What's weird about running the Old River Trail?" She stands with her hands on her hips. I've pissed her off, but I'm clueless as to how or why.

"No. Come on, you know that's not what I'm saying." I stand next to Margie, but not close. With her hands on her hips, her elbows stick out and fly back and forth with each turn. She's a weather vane in a mixed-up wind.

Margie's eyes are icy. She's madder now than she was the other day when I said she was cliché. "Really, Margie, what's wrong?" I want to know what's bugging her.

"Just forget it. Are we going to run the river or not?" Margie twists, twists, twists.

"Fine, if you want to run the loop trail we'll run it."

We stash Pedro and our bags back in the gym, then head out across the field. We start slowly, and I jog in small circles, in the center of the football field, taking in the woods, the school, and the clouds above. I love being in that space, seeing things from that perspective. It's like being in a boat in the middle of a lake. I hold my arms up to take in the sky.

Margie has jogged ahead of me. She hasn't said anything since we decided to run toward the woods. It is as though she has earbuds in her ears and she's lost in her own music world, except that there's no music.

"Margie, wait up." I pick up my pace. She steps it up a notch too. "You bum." My muscles are warm; I'm loose enough to open up my gait. Margie is warmed up, too, and she's running. Fast. She enters the woods. Even though I'm twenty feet or so behind her, I can hear her breathing and the spongy thud of footsteps on a beaten path—or is it my breathing and my footsteps?

"Margie! Wait!" She gets farther and farther ahead of me. "Come on! Margie!" I want her to stop, or slow down. She goes and goes and goes like water over a fall. "Slow down!"

The trees have closed their fingers against the light. It's dark once you leave the open field. My chest feels tight. I can't catch my breath. *Shh, shh, shh*, I focus on the sound, the wonderful sound of footfall after footfall.

"It's okay," I say to myself. "It's getting dark, but not too dark." I chatter to no one. "Margie just ran a little ahead. She'll stop any minute." I sound like a smoker gasping for breath. My heart aches. My feet weigh a thousand pounds each. I lumber on. I'm not a cat. I'm not smooth—each step is like my first one ever. I lurch forward, sputter like a jalopy running on empty. "Margie!" I'm so short of breath I can barely hear myself.

Then it happens. The earth gives way or was never there to begin with. When I finally find ground my body moves forward but my foot doesn't follow. It sounds like there's a gunshot and trees come alive with all the birds, deer, chipmunks, and mice fleeing at once. The entire wall

of woods rattles in front of me as I twist and fall. My vision blurs, I hit dirt, taste it. Pain runs up and down my
left leg like an electrical current determined to find an out-
let. My scream keeps running down the path. God, I hope
Margie hears it.

I hold my leg, try to pull myself back together, and
cry. Crying does not help. My leg hurts. Hurts, beyond
words. I've got to figure out how I'm going to get up, get
back, get home. Dirt, clumps of earth, fall from my hair.
Grit stings my eyes.

My whole leg, the ankle, calf, and knee, is turning
deep purple. It's grown wide and thick like a tree stump.
When I think about touching it, bolts of pain run from head
to toe and back. "It's okay. It's okay." Talk is the only balm
I have. I shake more dirt from my head and use the inside
of my t-shirt to wipe my face and wrap my shivering hands
close to my body.

"MARGIE!" Stupid, stupid Margie. The trees shoulder up one to the other and begin to erase what's left of
the light.

"All right, let's see if you can stand up," I order myself. I rise; hold my left leg out like a broken wing. Fire
consumes me. I scream so loud the trees bend. *Uhh, uhh,
uhh.* "Breathe, Andrea, breathe." Down I go. *Uhh, uhh,
uhh.* "Breathe." Again I rise. The scream is silent. The
trees, the sliver of sky, my body—all explode. I collapse.
Uhh, uhh, uhh. My lungs fight for every atom of oxygen.

I am a pile of snapped timber.

"MARGIE! HELP ME!" Like a rock overgrown by vines I can't move. "I need you," I tell the wind. My voice trails off. What am I going to do? How far did I run? Can I hop back? Is it shorter to go forward? I don't know what to do. "MARGIE!" The forest is a sponge that sops up my yells before they are halfway down the trail.

I stand up again. My leg sends drills of pain up through my back and head when my foot comes within three inches of touching ground. My foot says, "Don't even think about it!"

"Just one step," I command. My leg cries, yells, wails in protest. "Just one," I repeat. I approach the ground with my rotten stump of a leg. *Uhh, uhh, uhh.* Again I chew earth, collapsing, a shivered limb. My stomach churns with screams.

I need to find something to support myself. I do a three-legged crab walk toward the edge of the path. "A stick—" My leg kills. "I need a stick." *Uhh, uhh, uhh.* I move not at all, yet need to stop and rest. I cry. I imagine my dad waving at me from the trail head. "C'mon, kiddo, just six more inches." That helps me to scuttle farther, but not much. I can't go on.

What would happen if I didn't move another inch? Would I sleep? Die? Or gasp and heave from hunger and thirst? I wrap my arms around my shoulders and rock back and forth. I don't want to admit it—but I want my mom. My old mom. The one who picked me up the time I fell off my bike. Scooped me up like I weighed no more than a bundle of feathers. She hugged me close, rocked me, and sang away all the cold and pain. I want Mom.

"C'mon, kiddo, just one inch." I must move. It's slow going. I stop every few feet, or inches. Each time I do, tears run down my cheeks and along the edge of my chin. When I start to shiver and shake I know I need to move again. Despite all the trees and branches taunting me from above, I can't find a stick to save my life.

I'm doing my scrabble back down the trail toward the school, but it'll be midnight before I reach the football field. This isn't good. Every move I make, every breath I take is pain—pure pain.

I've got to hand it to the worm. It isn't easy getting from here to there when moving by centimeters. I can make it several feet now before I have to rest. But with each stop the desire to quit is stronger. It hurts too much, I'm not getting anywhere, I'm tired—this is the litany of blah, blah, blah that runs through my head. "MARGIE!"

"Get up. Hop." I continue to order myself around. Thankfully, grammar school jump rope developed my sense of balance, and one-legged skip rope built up my strength. I never, ever, thought I would make use of those skills.

Shh, shh, shh. I remember the cadence of running. It helps keep my mind off of the white-hot river running up and down my leg, through my back and head.

How is it that I'm in a forest and unable to find a stick? Twigs are everywhere, but crutch-sized branches are few. Beyond this evergreen, poking through the underbrush, I think I see one. If I could jump for joy I would. All I need to do is get through the ferns and past the tree and the stick is mine. With each hop my breath expels in a short burst. When I land I "*uhh*." Bending over, I reach for the branch. It's right here. I've got it. I've got it. Pull! Pull it from the underbrush.

I can't. Pull! I can't. It's attached to a log or root or something. I'm not able to see what holds it, but I can't break it free. I want to kick something. "SHIT!" I scream. The birds fly. I pull and pull. It will not let go. "SHIT!"

"Forget it!" I've got to move on. "Leave it." With every hop toward home I look back, wondering if I could just pull harder. "Don't," I tell myself. "Forget it."

There's another branch. This one is smaller and bent but it has give. It supports me as well as it can. This crooked stick doesn't take away pain, but it keeps me from falling. My pace picks up; for the first time I think I might escape the dark and dampened wood.

Light has faded; I can hardly see anything in front of me. Branches grab and poke at me, laughing. Their fingers scratch. When the sun goes down the forest sheds its sweet pine and extends its claws. It yanks at my shirt, my hair, my arms and legs. It's determined not to let me go.

"Andrea! Andrea!"

The voice is an echo, rising high into the air. I must be nearing the entrance to the trail. I'm sure people will wonder why I don't answer, why I don't yell, "Over here! Over here!" Samantha will want to know, most of all. I'll say it was because I was out of breath, I didn't hear people calling. Or I'll say that I did respond; I did call back. The truth is that when I hear my name being called I lose my voice. "Uhh, uhh, uhh," is all that I am able to say.

CHAPTER 9

"Andrea—Oh my God!" Margie runs to me. "What happened?" She approaches but stands back. "You okay?" Her voice is a high note. I can tell she wants to move in, to offer me a hand, but she holds back. She knows that I need space; she knows me better than anyone else.

"I waited for you. By the river." Margie bends over to meet me in my hobble. "Oh, Andrea—" She reaches out her hand. "—Please let me help you. Please?" She moves in close so her shoulder is within reach.

I want to keep walking. Walk as though Margie isn't there. Hop, crawl, or stumble back to school—that's what I want to do. But Margie, the Margie I know, the one who isn't mad at me, is standing right next to me and I can use her help.

Without saying a word I straighten, throw my stick into the woods and put my arm over her shoulder. This is so much easier. Together we emerge from the woods. The sky disappears into night, moon lights the grass. Margie's face is green; I wonder if mine is, too.

I sit on the wall and Margie hurries to the pay phone

outside the gym. Just once I'd like to be the one running for help.

The school is locked and we're in our exercise clothes so Margie dials 911. Dad's working tonight but he doesn't "catch" the call. The operator who answers can't put him on, since he's handling another emergency. But she knows her job. Fifteen minutes later Margie's mom shows up.

I hang onto Margie; hop toward the car when her mom arrives. I'm a problem that has to be dealt with and I don't like it. "Hi, Mrs. Williams," I speak to the ground.

"Your father's meeting us at the emergency room." Mrs. Williams opens the car door and helps me scoot and slide into the seat. "What happened?" She sits me up front. I'd prefer the back, the way, way back.

"Mom—drive." Margie is quick into the back seat. "Can't you see she's hurting?" Margie always gives her mother a hard time. It's the one subject she and I can't talk about without getting into an argument. Typically, Margie will sigh long and loud and tell me that I don't under-stand—just because her mother is sane doesn't mean it's easy being her daughter. When she says that, I usually stomp out of the room and bang the door as I go. Guess I won't be doing any stomping now.

"Are you okay?" Mrs. Williams helps me with my seatbelt. We start to pull away from the school.

"My leg hurts, a little." I don't want to belabor the crush in my leg. I don't want to talk at all. I wish Dad had been able to pick us up. Despite the heat in the car, I start to shake. I'm freezing cold. My teeth chatter.

The last thing I hear is Margie yelling, "Mom! Mom!" She sounds scared. "MOM!" I wonder what she's so afraid of.

I wake up in a hospital bed. I hear coughs, retching, and slow moans.

I'm floating. I don't feel any pain. I can't feel anything—not my legs, my feet, my toes—not anything.

"I had this dream," I say, "I wasn't in Kansas anymore, but you were there, and you, and you—and Toto, too." Dad looks at Mrs. Williams, Margie looks at my dad, everyone looks at everyone and then they all fade to black. I wonder, was Mom there, too?

I wake up and see my mom sitting at the end of the bed. She's twirling her hair with one hand and staring out a window that isn't there. She's counting, "One, two, don't let me get to three. One, two, don't let me get to three. One, two—" "—Mom!" I interrupt. That's all I say before the room disintegrates again.

✍

I wake up in the same hospital bed—at least it seems to be the same one. People have changed positions. I don't see Mrs. Williams, just Dad and Margie. "I loved running," I say, then whimper like a wounded dog. Both my dad and Margie move in closer when I speak. Dad looks like the Man on the Moon—his face is round and white, floating in a sea of black. Margie is Mars with her red hair. The two of them are here and then they're gone.

✍

This time it's like waking after a long, long nap. The room is colder. "Can I have another blanket?" My throat is the texture of sand.

Dad jumps up from the chair next to the bed. "Sure, sure, kiddo. I'll go get one from the nurse."

"I'll get it, Mr. McKane." Margie slips between the layers of curtain. "Be right back."

"What time is it?" I ask.

"It's a little after 10:00, not too late." Dad looks scruffy, like he's been sitting by my bed forever.

"My leg is killing me."

"I'm not surprised. You fractured it *and* sprained it. That must have been some stride."

The IV tube taped to the back of my hand itches.

"Actually it was the hole that was impressive." I'm not funny, so I don't know why I'm making jokes. There's a throbbing explosive pain in my leg, yet, the tape on the back of my hand is what bothers me most.

Dad's mouth turns up a little at the ends, but I can't say that he smiles.

"Don't look so worried. I'm going to live, right?" I'm wisecracking because I've got to cheer Dad up. My heart can't take it if I make him sad.

"Yeah, you'll live. I'm not so sure about that hole though. I'm liable to go out there and shoot it myself."

"You don't like guns, remember?"

"Oh yeah, there's that." Dad runs his hand through his invisible hair. It's weird how I can't see that Dad is bald, any more than he can.

"Dad, was Mom here?"

There is a pause, a wait, a stride.

"Uhh, no." Dad squints at me. He looks confused. "You know, right, that she couldn't come—even if she wanted to."

I can tell Dad has realized that he's said too much. "I called her though. Told her you were okay."

There is a pause, a wait, a stride.

"She sends her love." Dad runs his fingers through his pretend hair.

"Knock. Knock." The curtain flumps as Margie hammers at the makeshift door.

"Who's there?" I ask.

"Warmth," she says, waving a white blanket between the privacy layers.

"Come in. Come in," Dad and I say together.

"They cooked it," Margie says, handing the blanket to Dad.

"Oh, this is great." Dad spreads it out, covering me from neck to toe, except for my bum leg.

"Yeah, this feels good." I lift the blanket to my face, soaking up the heat. "Thanks, Margie."

The drugs must be wearing off because my leg is burning. I remember falling, and crawling, and Margie finding me.

"Thanks for helping me. Earlier." I point to my leg.

"I'm so sorry I ran ahead." Margie picks at the edge of the blanket. "Does it hurt?" She points at my leg. Tears brim her eyes. I'm making all the happy people sad.

"It's starting to. Those drugs wore off," I answer. "But don't worry. I'm okay."

Margie drops a tear and smiles at the same time. It is good to see a Margie grin. We have stuff to talk about, but we're still best friends.

There is talking in the hallway, and then the doctor enters.

"Ah, you're awake. How's the pain?" The doctor is wearing green hospital scrubs and the expected white coat.

"My leg hurts—" I look at my dad. "It's bad."

Dr. Stephens, according to her name tag, leans against the counter, crosses her legs. "I bet it hurts. You've got a serious fracture." She pulls a prescription pad from her pocket. "I'll give you something for the pain." She hands a piece of paper to Dad. "I'm sending you home with a removable walking cast, an Air Walker. Do not put pressure on your foot—none—until you can do so without feeling pain." Doc crosses her arms and gives me the stare. "Got it?"

I nod, repeatedly. This doctor means what she says.

"Until the swelling goes down, remove the cast daily to ice the leg. That's why I'm giving you a removable cast—ice." The doctor tugs the stethoscope draped around her neck as though it's a sweat towel and she's in the gym. "Andrea, I want to impress upon you that this break is severe. I'm hoping surgery won't be necessary, but we'll have to watch how you heal."

I nod some more and swallow several times.

"The nurse will bring you the air boot and crutches. You're set to go. If you have any questions, just call."

"Thanks, Doc," I say.

"You're very welcome. Watch your step on your way out."

With that, Dr. Stephens winks at me and leaves.

At the hospital, everyone's a comedian.

CHAPTER 10

Mom, a picture of her, plays peek-a-boo with me. The photograph, of Mom and me, is partially hidden by the things surrounding me on my bed. Each time Margie jostles the bed, Mom's face, laughing, pops out from underneath my first report card, a crayon drawing of Mom, Dad, and me, and the other silly stuff from my past.

I remember the photo, every detail of it, but pick it up anyway. In the picture Mom is laughing, her face bright. I'm laughing, too. We're wearing bathing suits and playing in a small plastic pool in the backyard. She blew bubbles in the water, on my belly, and I did the same for Pedro. It was before she got sick; before I knew to be afraid.

"I don't know what to put in the box." I toss the picture back on the pile of ticket stubs and pressed flowers and other stuff I've kept stashed in my drawer or taped to my mirror.

"Oh, this is a great picture. You should definitely put it in the box." Margie scootches over, picks up the picture, and holds it up for me to take.

"Uh. Try not to move so much." Every time Margie

moves, even if it is just a little bit, my leg, propped up on pillows, screams at me to stay still.

"Oh, sorry. Is the pain getting any better?"

"Not much. It still hurts—a lot. And I hate being stuck in bed." I snatch the picture from Margie.

"I can't imagine." Margie nudges the memento box even closer.

"This photo makes me want to cry." I lean back on the pillows, stare at the ceiling.

"Yeah, it's a happy-sad one." Margie pulls at my shirt-sleeve. "C'mon, back to work. I promised your dad I'd keep you busy so you wouldn't—'ruminate.'" She digs into the other keepsakes scattered about.

"What's this?" She picks up a bent, red, construction-paper heart.

I whistle, well, try to whistle a couple of notes. I raise my eyebrows and blow an empty column of air. "Hmm, apparently I don't tell you *everything* that happens to me." I need to stop moving my head; even that causes spikes of pain to run up and down the left side of my body.

"Well, I'll be. Ms. Andrea has a secret heart from a secret admirer." Margie waves the heart back and forth in front of me. "I demand to know more. Talk, McKane."

"Okay, okay." I hug a pillow to my chest to stifle the nausea activating in my stomach. I wish the pain would let me be. "Make yourself comfortable and I'll tell you the story of me and Eddie Weasel."

"You're making that up. The maker of this heart was not named Weasel."

"Sad but true."

"Spill." Margie moves slowly but it still kills. She sits up and grabs a pillow to hug herself.

"Eddie Weasel was my first love."

"What? How could you have a first love that I don't know about?" Margie starts to come up out of her cross-legged sit and stops. "Oops, sorry," she says.

I guess it is difficult for her as well—not being able to move around me the way that she used to. Again, I lean my head back on the pillow and close my eyes—this is what I do whenever there is a surge of pain.

"You okay?" Margie says.

"Yep." I take one deep breath, then another. The wave passes. "So where was I?"

"You just got started. You were going to tell me about the tall, dark, and handsome Eddie Weasel." Margie leans in just a little.

"Ah, I'm not so sure about tall. How tall are third graders?"

"Dark and handsome?"

"Would you believe blond, buck teeth, and freckles?" I cover my face with my pillow, pretending I'm too embarrassed to continue. "My knees went wobbly when he was near."

Margie laughs. "Your first love sounds—adorable," she says, pulling the pillow down from in front of my face.

Margie had placed the heart back on the pile of things. I pick it up and examine it. Getting heart curves to be smooth is so difficult. I can tell Eddie tried. More seriously, I say, "He was cute. At least those of us who liked boys and didn't think they had cooties, thought so."

"So did you kiss him?"

"No—"

"No?"

"No." I shake my head. "But he did kiss me." I can't believe I'm drawing out this story as though something exciting happened.

"On the lips?"

"Yep, right smack on the lips."

"The first kiss—it sounds sweet." Margie kicks out her feet and settles on her back, staring at the ceiling. "How come I don't have a 'first love' story? Where's my paper heart?"

"Yeah, where's your declaration of love?" I toss the heart at Margie—it goes up, then drops to the bed as though it hit an invisible wall. I'm not sure if I'm seeing correctly, the pain meds make things blurry sometimes, but it looks like Margie is crying. "Hey, what's wrong?"

"Nothing." Margie wipes tears from the sides of her face.

"Nothing? What do you mean?" Panic is bubbling up through my throat; my voice is squeaky. "Are you upset because you didn't get a paper heart from a Weasel?"

Margie turns her green eyes toward me—they look fierce. "Guys are always interested in you, and you don't even care about them." She turns away from me, lets go of her stare. "I do care, and they don't even notice me."

"What guys are interested in me? Eddie Weasel? Jimmy Moore? You can hardly call those guys 'guys.'" My leg registers every heartbeat with a burst of fire.

Margie turns to me again. This time she is glaring.

"You're talking about Sean? You're mad that Sean said 'Hi' to me?" I know that Margie isn't upset about Sean saying hi—I'm being a putz right now.

Again she releases her stare; this time though I feel more bad than angry. My leg starts throbbing—it wants me to be nicer to Margie. Breathe, one, two, three.

"Margie, please don't be mad at me. Matthew's going to fall head over heels for you. I know he will." I pick Pedro up off my bedside table, where he has been watching me with wide eyes of disapproval. He wants me to be nicer to Margie, too.

"I saw Matthew in the hall, the other day before we went running." Margie turns over, gently, so she's lying on her stomach, propped on her elbows. Even though she's careful not to jostle the bed, still my leg complains.

I keep my focus on Pedro to give Margie space, the way Samantha does with me.

"He didn't even see me. Didn't even nod, or smile or anything. It was as though I were invisible." Margie rolls back onto her back. I didn't realize how restless Margie could be until I became immobile.

"That's why you were upset?" I peek at Margie, while flopping Pedro's ears.

"Yeah, I guess." Margie hugs a pillow to her chest. "It was my idea to join the track team to meet boys and right away it works for you. Me? It'll just help me get into college." She covers her face with the pillow. She's making a noise and I can't tell if she's laughing or crying—maybe a bit of both.

"Hey—" Even though it hurts, I reach over and tug at the pillow. "Matthew just didn't see you. Was he wearing his glasses? Maybe he's nearsighted."

Margie jerks up to a sitting position, the bed flumps, my leg screams, I grimace. "Oh, sorry. But you're right— he wasn't wearing his glasses."

"There you go." I relax my face, my shoulders, as much of me as I can.

"He wasn't wearing his glasses!" Margie repeats. She puts her hand on her butterfly necklace, over her heart. "I can't believe I didn't think of that."

"You can't think of everything." I grip my bed cover to help with the pain.

"Andrea—" Margie rubs the charm of her necklace as though it has magical powers. "I am so sorry." One tear makes its way down one cheek, then another down the other. "I've been insane with jealousy." She tilts her head forward so red curls hide her from view. "I ran ahead of you, and you broke your leg."

"It wasn't your fault." I grab a couple of Kleenex and hand them to Margie. "Please don't cry. It makes me want to cry, too."

Margie runs the butterfly back and forth on the chain, her eyes, like mine, still moist. "When Mom gave me this, she said I shouldn't worry about being plain—all butterflies start out as caterpillars. 'Be patient,' she said."

"You really should listen to your mom sometimes. I know she drives you crazy—" I hesitate, breathe in, breathe out. I wish I'd used a different word. "—but she loves you. And she's smart."

Margie laughs. I drink in her smile like a cup of hot chocolate on a stormy day.

"Remember, we're freshmen, and it's only October." Even though the extension sends fire through my leg, I press Margie's knee. "You aren't plain. Matthew just hasn't had a chance to get to know you yet."

There's a knock at the door. "Come in."

Dad opens the door, "Hey, kiddo, Sean's on the phone, are you taking calls?"

My eyes widen, as do Margie's.

"Sure, Mr. McKane, she'll take it." Margie gets up and takes the cordless from my dad, hands it to me. I hold it out in front of me like I don't know what to do with it. Margie puts her pinky and thumb to her mouth and ear, miming phone, then grabs Dad and escorts him out of the room. Oh yeah, it's a phone.

"Sean? Hi." I grab Pedro and clutch him to my chest, tug on his ear.

"Hi." Seconds pass like molasses through a straw. "I guess you didn't want to go running with me." Sean laughs. "At least you came up with a good excuse."

"I did want to go running with you. I did." I'm not sure what hurts more—packing my leg in ice or not being able to run with Sean. "I hate it that we didn't get to run together."

"Well, since running is out, how about the movies?" Sean's exhales are loud explosions. He must be holding the phone close to his face.

"Okay," I get a bubbly feeling, then remember that I'm on bed rest for three more days. "But I can't go anywhere yet." My voice fades to a whisper.

"Oh." Sean doesn't say anything for several long seconds. "How about next Saturday?"

"That'll work." I'm riding waves—happy, sad, happy. Pedro's ears flop up and down with each surge. "Saturday is good."

"Will you be in school on Monday?" Sean asks.

"Yeah. Finally." Happy, sad.

"Great. See you then."

"Okay."

"Cool. Okay." Sean sounds like he's been running. He exhales a few more bursts into the phone. "Bye."

"Bye. See you Monday." Reluctantly I hang up the phone. Since I can't jump up and down, which is what I want to do, Pedro takes a couple of hops for me.

"Margie!" I call. She comes right in, which tells me she was waiting just outside the door.

"Tell me. Tell me." She bounces on the bed. "Oh sorry. I forgot."

Breathe in, breathe out. Not even the pain can wreck how good I feel. "He asked me to go to the movies on Saturday." My leg hurts and I'm smiling from ear to ear.

Margie claps her hands. "That's great. What else?"

"That's it." I shrug my shoulders. "He'll see me in school."

"Oh Andrea, this is so cool." Margie goes to my closet, and one by one, pulls out shirts and dresses and skirts, and one by one puts them all back again. "We might have to go to the mall before Saturday."

"That should be an experience." My leg gets heavier with talk of movement. "Margie, I'm tired. Can we finish the box?"

"Sure. Where were we?" Margie returns to the bed, sits with hardly a bounce. She opens the box and puts it before me. "Which things do you want to put in it?"

"The Freedom medallion, for sure." It is just out of reach so Margie places it in the box for me. Even though everything is next to me on the bed, like a person with a stiff neck, I can't reach or twist enough to grasp these objects that are so close.

"Your wishing stone?" Margie holds up the water-worn gray rock with the cream white stripe running around the center. Dad gave me the stone a long time ago. I was supposed to make a wish and throw it over my left shoulder, but my wish was to keep it—so I did.

"Definitely." I nod at the rock and at the box. Bobbing my head like a chicken sends spasms up and down my back. I remind myself to use words.

"Grab me one of my running shoes, would you?" I point at my shoes that have been tossed haphazardly in the corner of the room. Margie hands me the sneaker, and I pull the lace out of it. The lace I put in the box myself, although my leg lodges yet another complaint. I breathe in and out—in, one, two, three; out, one, two three. "The picture of your mom and you?" Margie holds the picture, careful not to smudge the image. I take it from her and look again at the happy girl and her beautiful mother, at Mom and me.

"Mom was so funny." I circle my hand in the air. "She used to stir the water and say she was making kid soup. It cracked me up."

Margie doesn't move an inch. She may be holding her breath.

"Do you think she remembers the good times we had?"

"Sure she does." Margie scoots around, jostling some but not too much, so she can look at the photo with me.

"I hope she doesn't; that she can't. I think remembering would be hell." I pass my fingertips over the photo, barely touching the surface. My hands shake as though I'm in the cold of deep winter.

I place the photo in my box. "That's enough for now. I'm tired."

"Sure, sure." Margie collects the other items, careful not to tear a paper heart or knock a single macaroni off of the gold-painted pasta wreath I made for my mother ten years ago or so.

"Thanks, Margie." I close my eyes before I finish speaking. There is no thinking about it. Remembering *is* hell.

And tiring, too.

CHAPTER 11

Margie plops down in the seat next to mine in psych class. "Sooo," she wiggles her eyebrows, "how's Sean?"

"I can't believe you did that!" I grasp the edge of my desk like I'm holding on for dear life. "He's going to every class with me!" This is my first chance to scold Margie. Earlier she pawned me off on Sean. She was supposed to carry my books while I crutched my way from class to class. In typical Margie fashion, she finagled it so Sean is my sidekick instead. My voice is bright, a dead giveaway that I'm not really angry.

"Yeah, exciting, isn't it?" Margie asks.

I fold my arms across my chest, purse my lips—pretending I am so mad.

"Oh, cut it out." Margie tugs at my shirt-sleeve. "Tell me you aren't excited."

"Well—" I tap my finger to my lips. "There was a thing, an altercation. Something to do with Matthew Davidson." I pause, wait; I *hmm*. "That was—," I nod my head a few times, "—*exciting*."

"What altercation? What are you talking about?" Margie bounces in her seat.

"Oh, oh. Class is starting." I point my finger toward the front of the room. The way she's sitting Margie can't see Mr. Portland.

"McKane, I swear." Margie turns around. She flicks her pen back and forth—curiosity buzzes in her ear. I can tell.

Margie and I don't hang out with the students in psych class; they're all upperclassmen. Freshmen don't normally take Psychology, but Margie wanted to meet "older" boys, and I wanted to take it because—well, because of Mom. We are our own special clique of two in this class.

"Attention, young men and women—" Mr. Portland is a science guy. He always wears a suit and tie, with thick-rimmed glasses. It's funny that he teaches Social Psychology. "I need to go to the Principal's office for a few minutes." He sorts through papers on his desk. "Please review the Milgram experiment from last week and read the Harlow study for today." Chairs scrape, backpacks open, there is a mumble of activity.

As soon as Mr. P steps out of the room, Margie swivels around. "Tell me. Tell me." She puts both hands over my ancient copy of *Abnormal Psych* so I can't read it even if I want to.

I pitch forward over my desk, "Kevin 'Dimwit' told Michael that Matthew was queer and that's why he hangs around with freshmen." I whisper. "He said it just as Sean and I came around the corner."

"Oh, my God!" When Margie is surprised, her eyes get big, bigger, and biggest. She gets Pedro eyes.

"Sean told them off, though." I pull my book away from Margie. "What study are we supposed to read?" I flip a few pages.

"Andrea!" Margie yanks the book back from me and slaps it closed. "Right now. Speak!"

"Ruff. Ruff."

Margie's lips tense into a hard line. I'd better tell her, and quick. "Okay. Relax." Who am I trying to kid? I'm dying to relay what happened. "Sean told 'Dimwit' to shut up and grow up."

Margie sucks in air; she puts her hand over her open mouth. "But Sean is a freshman. Kevin is a senior!"

"I know. I know. Kevin called Sean a boy-toy." I don't think I make a sound—just mouth the words—that's how quiet I am.

"I don't believe it!" Margie leans toward me, concerned, the same way Samantha does in therapy. "What did he do? What did you do?"

"I didn't do anything. Sean pushed me past them. His face was all red—"

There is a clap of thunder outside. I shrink from the sound. "What the—?"

Margie pats the pages of my text; brings my attention back to her and away from the outdoors. "What did Sean say?"

In the short time we've been talking, a storm has snuck in from out of town. A ferocious wind rattles the classroom windows; it's desperate to find a way in. Gray clouds swirl, wrap themselves up and around each other. If storms didn't frighten me so much, I'd think they were beautiful.

"He said he was sorry." I turn a few more pages. "That those guys have some beef with Matt and they're idiots."

Margie looks out at the torrent of gray. "Why do guys act like jerks?"

"I don't know, maybe the answer's in here." Now I slap the pages of my book. "Let's look for an illness called 'Small School Syndrome.' The main symptom of it is it makes everyone get into everyone else's business."

There's another boom of thunder; my shoulders jolt to my ears and drop. I'm rarely the studious one, but right now I need to distract myself from the angry squall. "C'mon. Mr. P will be back any second," I say to Margie.

"Right." Margie takes her book and puts it on my desk. We leaf through last week's chapter and search for Harlow.

"I hated the Milgram study." I rub my arms like I'm cold. "People electrocuting other people because they don't know the capital of Montana or something."

"*Pretending* to electrocute." Margie corrects me.

Wind drives rain into the side of the school. It howls at every wall it meets. Breathe—one, two, three, I remind myself.

"I wonder what bizarre research Dr. Harlow has for us?" I find the correct section in the table of contents.

Margie slumps in her seat. "I read this one last night. It's sad." Despite all the energy she dedicates to boys and romance, Margie is a good student; she reads ahead and stays on top of the homework assignments. I'd be lost without her reminding me what we're doing and when it's due.

"Sum it up for me?" I learn best when Margie tells me something and then I read about it later.

"Well, these scientists—mad scientists if you ask me—took these adorable baby monkeys and put them in a cage with two monkey dolls." Margie turns the pages of her text. "One doll was made of wire with a soft cushy covering. The other was made of just wire, hard wire." Pages continue to turn one after the other.

"That's dumb. The monkeys liked the soft 'mom' better. Right?" There's another crack of lightning and rumble of thunder. The class *oohs* in response.

"They did. But the hard one had food and the soft one didn't." Margie runs her finger down one page, then the next.

Like a beating drum, thunder pounds at the roof. It threatens to break in.

"Don't tell me the babies starved." I push at my desk. Some of these studies make me want to get up, get out, to run. However, I go nowhere. My leg sticks into the aisle, a thrown anchor.

"I don't think they died. Any of them." Margie switches her book so it's facing me. "The ones that had food failed to thrive. The others were hungry." She points to a picture of an emaciated rhesus monkey, clutching a doll. "See? This baby clings to the cuddly mom even though it's starving."

I rear back. Lightning crackles. Rain falls, sounding like an avalanche of rocks. It doesn't let up. The baby rhesus is beyond sad. His ears stick out; his mouth is grim. He weighs nothing.

"Damn it!" Thunder quickens. "I've got to go." In the photo, I see a desperate monkey, tiny, clinging to its mom, eyes empty like wire circles. I see skinny arms wound around indifferent cloth. I see me. "The nurse—" I reach for my crutches but my movement is spastic and I knock them to the floor. I try to stand, but my body doesn't cooperate. I twist, there's killer pain, and I fall forward on top of a crutch. "Shit!" I say much too loudly.

"Jesus, Andrea, can't you even sit in a chair without falling?" James, Kevin's friend, laughs.

"Shut up, James!" Margie kneels by my side, takes hold of my upper arm. "Andrea, what happened?"

"Let go, Margie. Please, just let go." I don't know what I'm doing, or how to get up, so I crawl. I scuttle across the linoleum squares of the damn classroom, wishing I could vanish, or that I never was.

Margie collects my crutches and follows behind me. "*Please*. Let me help you." She sounds exasperated.

I extend my arm, giving Margie something to grip. She braces herself to provide support as I stand. It isn't that I'm heavy; it's my leg and cast that make it difficult for me to get up from the floor. Margie offers me my aluminum walking sticks. "I'll tell Mr. P you're at the nurse's office."

I hope I don't start crying. I swing and hop myself the rest of the way to the door, Margie watches me, the text remains open on my desk, and the starving monkey snuggles with the uncaring thing it thinks of as Mom.

"I'll bring your books over tonight." Margie takes a few steps toward me, only a few. "Later." She tilts her head. "You okay?" Only she would know that staying away is the kindest thing anyone could do for me.

"Yeah. I am. Really." I'm weak-kneed, unsteady on my feet. "It's just my leg. It hurts."

"Go." Margie urges me out of the room by flicking her wrist and returns to my desk.

There's another rumble of thunder and a snap of lightning. Margie slams the textbook shut and says, "Stupid scientists."

I turn and wobble out of the room. The rain hails against the roof, thunder rolls. I shiver at the sound. Today is a day that would make Dr. Frankenstein happy.

Chapter 12

"So, Andrea, how are you doing?" It's still raining, and more than anything I want to be home, in bed, listening to music, or reading, or doing something besides sitting here in Samantha's gray-blue office.

"I'm falling down a lot."

"Falling down?" Samantha's brow scrunches up. "Tell me what you mean."

"I fell down in Psychology today." I don't move a muscle. It's as though I myself am made of metal, like those monkeys.

"I'm not sure I understand. Did you black out? Trip?" Samantha leans forward as she always does.

"Forget it." Why do I say anything? I should stay quiet. "It's stupid." The egg on the side table captures my attention. A beautiful egg, painted around the middle. For the first time I can't concentrate on the floor. "Do you know about the study they did with baby monkeys, putting them with wire mothers?"

"Yes, I've read that study." Samantha settles back in her chair. "I'm trying to follow you, Andrea."

"What happened to that one monkey? The one that failed to thrive?" I quickly glance from the egg to Samantha, just to see what she's doing. The mood I'm in has ruined my ability to see things even when not looking. "You know, the one that had to live with the wire mom without any fur or anything?"

"I don't know. What do you think happened to it?"

"Oh come on, Samantha. Forget the therapist baloney." My attention returns to the egg; I cross my arms. "I wondered is all."

"Andrea, why don't you tell me what's going on?" Samantha presses her fingertips together—moves her palms in and out like a bellows.

"I'm sick of this place, that's what's going on." My good foot rat-a-tat-tats on the carpet —without making a sound. "I come here every week, sometimes twice a week, and nothing happens." I want to move my broken leg as well. "I sit here, and blah, blah, blah—it's the same old nothing every week." I wish I could go back to not speaking. With every word, the hole I dig gets bigger.

"Something happened today. Tell me what happened." Samantha has her elbows on her knees again as she leans toward me, somehow looking at the floor and at me at the same time.

"Does that make you some kind of genius, that you can tell something happened today? I've got news for you, something happens everyday. Every, frickin' day."

"Andrea, I'm going to stop you here." Samantha is like a traffic cop, forcing me to idle with her hand. "I'm concerned it will be difficult for you, later, if I let you act out your anger. Please, try to tell me why you are upset."

"I don't want to stop doing anything, and I'm not acting out! This is stupid. Therapy is stupid." I stand, or try to; I can't get up from the couch very well. When I stand, Samantha stands, too.

"Sit down." She puts her hand on my crutches so I can't move them. She's very still. Her lack of motion, for some reason, unbalances me and I drop back down onto the couch, like the rivers of rain falling off the eaves of the house next door.

"See, I told you I'm falling down a lot." I'm slouched so low, I'm almost horizontal on the couch. My arms are crossed, and my hair hangs over the front of my face. I blow at the strands to clear my view.

Samantha rests my crutches on the couch near me; takes her seat. "Let's try this again. What happened?"

It isn't easy to see it from my flattened position, but I find my favorite square in the carpet. Silence, sweet silence is everywhere in the room; outside, rain and wind raise a ruckus. Samantha waits.

"I'm asking again—what happened?" Seconds pass, her hands, her feet, her body are quietly waiting, they seem to be listening.

Samantha takes a deep breath in, lets it out. She waits. She listens. The downpour drowns out the silence between us.

"Listen, Andrea, your visit with your mother is this Sunday." She inches forward in her seat. "I want you to be in a good frame of mind." Another breath, in and out. "Please talk to me." She sounds frustrated.

Wind roars at the window. Even the storm is unhappy with me.

"My mother." I scratch my leg inside the top of my cast. "She's been sick for a long time."

Samantha waits; she nods, encouraging me to continue.

"I didn't know she was sick then, when I was younger. You know what I mean?" My leg itches. I can't quite reach the spot. "I thought she went crazy later, when I was older. But I remembered something." That was a dumb thing to say.

"What did you remember?"

Shh, shh, shh, I remember the sound of running.

"Andrea?"

Shh, shh, shh. Rain strikes at the glass. *Shh, shh, shh*. I've got to find words.

"I can't. I can't. I can't." *Shh, shh, shh*. My legs want to go. I grab a throw pillow and hug it to my chest. Why can't I forget the things that I remember? My left leg is concrete; it holds me in my seat. I twist and turn trying to break free, but go nowhere.

Samantha takes a deep breath in. "Talk to me, Andrea." She waits, leans forward, clearly she's thinking. The rain will not let up. "Tell me why you can't speak."

The rain is pelting the roof, the window, the side of the building. *Shh, shh, shh.*

"Andrea, can you tell me what's happening right now? Why you can't talk to me?"

Samantha's eyes look huge and her face distorted, as though she's looking at me through a peephole in a door. She moves in and out of my vision. First the color drains, then the light, then the only thing visible is Samantha's rubbery face in the imaginary pinhole.

"Because—" Get up. Get out. I'm like a beetle on its back, scrabbling. "Because—"

"Andrea?" Samantha asks.

I close my eyes so I don't see the awful image that is now her face.

"Help me—" Getting up I grab my crutches and take a step without first putting a crutch under each arm. I go down again. "Help me—please," I say from the floor.

"I will." Samantha extends her arm. The room is still in motion, rising and falling in waves of dark and light. "I want to," she says.

I use Samantha's arm to support me as I rise to an awkward crouch—one leg straight, the other bent. "Okay," I say, although I'm not sure why. Samantha helps me to the couch. I hop. I fall. Landing in the seat, I grab a pillow and hug it close. Back and forth I rock.

"I had to do it." Back and forth.

"Do what?"

"She said she'd kill Dad." I drop the pillow and cover my ears. I can't stand that sound. I can't stand the horrible crying. "Help me!" Back and forth. My eyes are shut so tight not one atom of air can get through and the tears cannot escape. Maybe I'll drown. "Help me—please."

"It's okay." Samantha gets up and pours a glass of water. She places it on the table next to me. "You're okay." She scoots her chair closer to mine. "Tell me, what did you have to do to keep your father safe?"

Shh, shh, shh. "I tried to run, but she grabbed me." My eyes are open, I look for Samantha—everything is blurry as I peer through deep water.

"Your mother grabbed you and made you do something?"

I nod. The room flickers from dark to light. The storm howls.

Samantha waits.

"I had to put the—"

Samantha waits.

"I put the kitten, my kitten, Tigger—"

"It's okay, Andrea, really it's okay." Samantha leans further forward. She's close.

"I put Tigger in the chest—in my toy box." My hands shake, my good leg bounces, my left leg shivers with pain. "I didn't want to. It was raining, and Tigger put paw prints on the floor."

"Breathe in and out. Take your time, you're doing great."

It's difficult to talk while swallowing words and tears, but I keep trying. "She went crazy over the paw prints. She said she was going to kill him."

"Breathe, Andrea, breathe."

"I told her no. I wish I had never said anything, but I said 'No! He's my kitty.'" I look at Samantha. I want to know if she knows what happens next. Maybe I don't need to make another sound. I bite my lip.

"It's important that you say it," she says.

I shake my head from side to side, resisting and speaking at the same time.

"When I said no, Mom laughed. She said I was right. She wasn't going to kill Tigger—" My fingers stroke the pillow in my lap. "I was." The corduroy makes light and dark stripes with every swipe of my hand—black, white, black, white, I work the pillow so it looks like an SOS beacon.

"I tried to run. I didn't know what else to do. But she grabbed me, lifted me up, even." I sit up, my spine straightens like a rod, I raise my arms. "My legs were running in the air. 'You think you're so smart,' she said." I wave my hands like they are frantic feet. "'Put the cat in the box, or I'll put you in there!' Mom yelled." I drop my hands, my shoulders, my head. Without looking, I watch Samantha.

"I'm right here. You're safe." Samantha is still, quiet. She gives me space and stays near. "What happened next?"

"I said, 'Go ahead! Put me in the box.'" The room swirls like cream in a cup of coffee. "Samantha, I'm going to be sick." My shoulders rattle up and down.

Samantha places her wastebasket near my foot. "It's okay if you get sick." She gets a dish towel from her closet and places it next to me on the couch. I pick it up and wrap it around my hands—I need to stop the punches that build up inside.

"Did your mother put you in the box?"

"Mom said I'd die before she'd let me out of the box. I told her I didn't care." I'm shaking my head, rocking—more restless than Margie has ever been.

"What happened then?"

I look at Samantha. I see Tigger. I see the baby rhesus. I see me.

She waits.

My mouth turns in on itself. My lips defy me to utter another word. Say it, don't, say it, don't. "Say it" wins.

"She'd done some crazy things, but she'd never been like this." I yank at the towel wrapped around my fists. "She screamed that I was miserable, rotten, awful, just like my father." I twist my hands. "She hit me."

"Breathe."

I inhale. "Mom dragged me around the house by the back of my shirt looking for Tigger. We had to find him. He'd run away." I stop and take a few deep breaths over the wastebasket, spit once, then twice.

I look at Samantha, plead with my eyes to let this be over.

"You're doing great. Don't forget to breathe."

I take a deep breath in. "When we found him, she jerked me in front of her and grabbed both my wrists like I was a puppet. She made me pick Tigger up, then pulled us, Tigger and me, back to my toy box. 'Put him inside! Get rid of the ugly, dirty thing!' she screamed."

I spit a few more times.

"Sounds awful," Samantha whispers.

"I stood there, holding Tigger. His little paws still had mud on them. I tried to wipe it off, but he didn't like anyone touching his feet." Spit, drink some water, spit. "It's really cold in here," I say through chattering teeth.

Samantha gets a blanket from the closet and drapes it around my shoulders.

"Mom lifted the lid on the box. 'Put him in there, you despicable—.' She called me a bad name." The rain is coming down in sheets. I want the rain to stop.

"Samantha—"

"Go ahead. It's okay."

"I— I— I put Tigger in the box." Again, I cover my ears and tighten into a small rock. I don't want to hear or smell or see. "Mom slammed the lid shut. I tried to open it back up. Tigger was crying. His meow was so loud. When I tried to open the box, Mom went even more berserk."

Back and forth I rock. I feel like I'm in that box; everything is dark, not even a dusting of light.

"She lifted me up by my shirt or my neck or something. She shook me and said, 'You ever disobey me again, I'll kill you. I'll kill you and your father too!'" *Shh, shh, shh.* Despite the pain, my broken leg agitates to run. "Then she tossed me on the floor and yelled at me to go to my room—but we were in my room. I climbed on my bed because I didn't know what to do."

"And Tigger?"

"I don't feel good, Samantha." Spit, spit. Bile rises in my throat.

"I know you don't. You're doing great, though. Can you tell me what happened to Tigger?"

"He was meowing and scratching at the box. For hours he cried." I pull the blanket tight around my shoulders. "I wanted to die, to kill myself. Do anything to make the crying stop." Back and forth I rock. "I just hid under the covers, put a pillow over my head, and hoped someone would help me, or Tigger, or kill us both." I throw up air into the basket.

"I must have fallen asleep or something, because when I came to, the scratching and yowling had stopped. I thought Tigger was dead." My shoulders shake as I cry, tears fall on my shirt, the couch, the carpet.

"Yes," Samantha says. "You were heartbroken."

My body, the whole of it, nods in agreement.

"I got up from my bed and went into the kitchen." Like water in a kettle, words are boiling in my throat. "My mother was holding Tigger up to her face, petting his head. She brushed her cheek against his and said, 'Some people are so mean. Don't you worry, Tigger. I won't let anyone hurt you. You're my little kitty.' Tigger licked her face."

With that, I vomit lunch into the wastebasket. Samantha moves my crutches so she can sit next to me on the couch. She rubs my back as I finish throwing up.

"I'm sorry. I'm so sorry," I say between spits.

"Sorry about what? You don't have anything to be sorry about."

"For earlier, and for puking in your office." I laugh, I cry; I feel like I'm covered in snot and vomit. Samantha laughs, too.

"It's okay, my office can take it." She pulls back the curtain of hair that covers my face.

Tears run down, jumping from my chin to my lap. "I miss Tigger."

Samantha tilts her head in a question. "Dad gave him away." My fingers claw the air. "He scratched the furniture, and Mom was upset."

Samantha nods. "I'm so sorry, Andrea."

"Yeah." The room is heavy, sinking, darkening. "I'm really tired. Can I lie down for a minute?" I start to lie down—fall, really—without even waiting for an answer. My broken leg sticks out from under the blanket like a goofy kickstand. Sleep wants to take over.

Samantha pulls the blanket up over my shoulders. "You can rest for awhile. You're my last client today. I should go tell your dad, though. He's probably waiting for you."

My eyes open wide, I try to sit up. "No! Please don't tell my dad!"

"I'm going to tell him that you're resting, that's all. So he doesn't worry."

"Oh. Yeah, that makes sense." Sleep returns to lower me onto the couch, to rest my head on the pillow. "He's probably out front in the car." The sound of rain becomes a lullaby.

"You are a brave girl, Andrea. You did great today."

I'm not at home, in bed, listening to music or reading, yet I'm more relaxed than I have been in months. The wind and rain batter at the shingles, and I sleep as though the sun is shining, the birds are singing, and Pedro is standing guard.

CHAPTER 13

"Let me get this straight. You overheard Sean and Matthew saying they were eating at Dino's?" Leaning on my crutches, I push shirts, one right after the other, to the right on the clothes bar. "And that's why we're going there?" Nothing grabs my attention.

"That's right." Margie pulls a strange blue shirt off of the rack. It is dark blue with a bright green crisscross pattern on one side. "What do you think of this?" She holds the shirt up, the wire of the hanger, in my opinion, lifted too close to her eye.

"Eww. Are you serious?" I shake my head. Honestly, I hope she's joking with me.

"What's the matter, McKane? You don't like a little neon chicken-wire printed on your chest?" She puts the shirt back in the rack.

Her question doesn't even warrant an answer. "Uh, let's back up. Tell me again, why are we going to Dino's when Sean and Matthew are likely to be there?" It was a big deal getting out and going to the mall, but I didn't dress up or anything. I didn't expect to see Sean. For Margie the reason to go to Dino's is, for me, the reason not to go. It's as though we're speaking two different languages.

Margie pulls out a sable-colored, scallop-necked shirt. It's simple but it will look beautiful on her. "That's a keeper," I tell her.

"You think so?" She goes to the mirror, holds out a sleeve with one hand, the neck and hanger with the other. "It does look nice." She turns from side to side. "God, I hate my body."

That's one reason I don't find any new shirts or skirts to wear. I don't want to confront, in the mirror, my log for a leg, crutches, flat chest, and long, stringy hair.

"Cut it out." I think Margie is beautiful and fits her body perfectly.

The sleeve of this magenta turtleneck is deliciously soft. I'd try it on, except every action is difficult—changing clothes, washing, walking, waving—everything. If my leg wasn't broken, and I didn't have crutches, and I could stand, I'd try on this shirt and a skirt or two. As it is, I push it and all the other pieces on the rack over to the right.

"I hate my body more," I hobble up behind Margie and stand up straight on my one good leg. "And with good reason." I copy Margie's twisting motion, turning on my metal wings like I'm a spiral staircase.

"My mom says, 'All teenage girls hate their bodies.' That it's just a sad part of being a teenager." Margie slides a few more shirts out of the way, but I'm glad she's set the brown one aside.

"Again, your mother has said something really smart. I don't know why you say she's so stupid." I take a blue and an orange shirt off the rack to my right and hand them to Margie for her to try on.

"Alright. Maybe she's smart sometimes." Margie holds up an orange blouse with a small red flower print, "What do you think of this one?"

I squint my eyes, wrinkle my nose, and shake my head no. "I think the brown one is the best."

"Yeah. Me too."

I back up, as awkward as that is for me, and give Margie the space to return the other shirts to their racks.

"Aren't you going to try something on?" Margie asks.

"No. I feel too much like that ugly teenager. Which is why, Ms. Williams, I can't believe we're meeting up with the guys!"

Margie holds a couple of the shirts she was in the process of returning up against my chest.

"Don't even get that blue-and-green thing near me." Standing on one foot, I lean a crutch against my side and hold my hand up to fend her off.

"Okay, not the blue-and-green." She slides another shirt back onto a nearby rack. "Let's look at the jewelry."

I hop toward the display cases up front. I don't wear jewelry very often, or, better said, never. It's too flashy for me, draws too much attention to my gawky self. I like picking pieces out for Margie though—earrings and neck-laces look great on her.

"Ooh. This one will go great with that brown shirt." I point at a polished round rock, cut with a hole in the middle and a thin leather cord serving as the necklace. The stone has green, brown, and orange speckles.

"That's beautiful." Margie taps her nail against the glass of the case. "Excuse me," she says to the woman behind the counter. "Could I try this on?"

"Sure. Sure." The counter lady, who wears too much pink, snaps gum, and walks as though her feet hurt, minces her way over to our section. "This one? This one?" She moves her hand from necklace to necklace waiting to be told to stop.

"That's it," Margie says.

"Oh this is beautiful. Just beautiful." Ms. Pink holds the necklace up like a game-show gift presenter. She's not lying though; it is beautiful.

Margie reaches behind her neck and fiddles with the clasp of her butterfly necklace. She takes it off and hands it to me. "I want you to put this in your wooden box—for awhile at least." Margie holds the thin silver chain so it sways; a silver butterfly, wings wide, hanging at the bottom of the curve.

"What?" I bat at the air in front of her hand. "I can't take your butterfly."

"I want you to have it, at least until your mom comes home." She bounces her hand in a "*take it, take it*" gesture. "Whatever good advice my mom has for me, applies to you."

"You want me to put this in my memento box?" I lift the butterfly so it doesn't strain against the chain.

"Just for awhile. While we're doing our caterpillar stuff." Margie's eyes are a glittering green like the ocean on a warm summer day.

"Really?"

"Yes, McKane! Take it, already." She doesn't actually drop it, forcing me to scoop it out of freefall, but she comes close. "C'mon, I want to try on this new one." Margie smiles at Ms. Pink.

"I'll wait. No hurry," Ms. Pink says, although it is easy to see that her arms are tired of holding out the stone and she's ready to move on to something else.

I lift the necklace off of Margie's fingers. "Thanks. I'll take good care of it." And I do. I slide it into my breast pocket, where it will be safe and close to my heart.

"Good. Now this." Ms. Pink jabs the polished rock at Margie.

Margie loops the leather over her head. It's long enough to wear without undoing the clasp. It is gorgeous on her.

"Wow. That looks great." I take one swing back on my crutches to see from farther away. "You look fantastic." Truth is, I'm stunned by how beautiful Margie is. It's as if this is the first time I've ever seen her.

"Okay, don't overdo it." Margie lifts the necklace off her neck to check the price.

"Listen to your friend. She knows." Ms. Pink snaps her gum several times.

"You've got to get that." I pull my wallet out of my jacket pocket. "I'll give you my clothes money."

"It's inexpensive. Quite cheap." Ms. Pink writes numbers on her pad of paper. "Just $20.28."

Margie and I exchange glances. "She'll take it," and "I'll take it," we say in unison. Margie buys the brown shirt, too.

I don't know much about the life cycles of butterflies, except that they go from caterpillars to chrysalis to gorgeous adults with their whole lives written on their wings in bold colors. With my broken leg, I feel every bit the caterpillar, slow to make my way.

Margie, though, as she put on that necklace, and it brought out the green of her eyes and the red of her hair and the rose of her skin, has spread her wings.

I don't feel bad that Margie is ahead of me, growing up more quickly. Because watching her, I know what's possible. And standing here, awed by my friend, I know that there are wings wrapped from my toes, up around the pendant near my heart, to the top of my head. One day they'll open and spread out and out and out until they touch the horizon.

CHAPTER 14

"How do I look, Dad?" I tried on a dozen different outfits, and every change required hopping and balancing and one too many falls. I wanted to find something that worked well with a knee-high orthopedic boot. I settled on a jeans skirt and a crew-neck, long-sleeved shirt under a yellow sweater. I look horrible.

"Wow! kiddo, you look beautiful." Dad sounds shocked. I don't know if that's a good thing or not. "What did you do with my little girl? You know, the little one with the ponytail, braces, and knobby knees?"

"Cut it out, Dad. I'm serious." I give Dad my most intense thin-eyed glare. "And when Sean comes to the door, don't interrogate him or anything." I don't want Dad being a goof when he meets Sean.

I've been sharp with Dad since my meltdown in Samantha's office. I don't mean to be. I'm on edge because I can't tell him what happened. When I try, no words come out.

"I don't know how I feel, you going out with this boy when— well, when you're a young woman, for gosh sakes." His voice splinters and he runs his hand over his head.

"Dad." I hobble over to him. "You'd better not be worried."

He coughs, speaks through a garbled voice, then coughs again. "No, kiddo, I'm not—" he loses his voice again, "—I'm not worried. It's just that you've grown up so much." He has tears in his eyes. "You look like your mother did when I first met her."

Oh no, don't say that. And don't start sobbing—I can't deal with that.

"Dad, please don't cry. Not when Sean will be here any minute." As I say the words, tears roll down my cheeks. "See! This is what I mean." I hurry into the bathroom expecting to see mascara running in lines down my face. I love Dad, but he's too sweet.

"Sorry, kiddo, I'm better now," he calls after me. "Really, you can come out. No tears, I promise."

"I hope not." I raise my voice at the door. I'm not mad, but I can't be nice, either. In the mirror I see my mother's face. My eyes are gray, hard as sharp stone. I don't know what Dad's talking about when he says I'm beautiful; I'm the essence of ugly.

There's a knock at the front door.

"Damn it!" I dab water on my face and pinch my cheeks. That's some crazy torture Margie told me about. It's supposed to make you look healthy and alive. I think I look pinched. It's time to snap out of my mood.

I hear Dad open the door and welcome Sean inside. I grab my crutches and exit the bathroom as quickly as I can. "Sorry, Dad, we have to go. Sean's mom or dad must be waiting in the car." I kiss Dad on the cheek, grab my coat and shove it between the poles of my crutch, hop over a few steps, and open the front door.

"It's my brother—" Sean says, looking at the floor, at my dad, and at the floor again. "My brother's driving us."

"Your brother?" Dad follows Sean and me as we step outside. "How old is he?" Dad bends over to get a side-long look into the car idling on the street.

"He's twenty. He works at the newspaper." Sean is talking over his shoulder to my dad and walking to keep up with me. I hurry.

"It's okay, Dad," I call, and wave as Sean opens the car door. "He's old enough."

"Sure. Okay, you two. Have a good time."

I can't help myself. I turn and watch my dad, standing in the doorway and waving goodbye as we drive off.

"Your dad is nice," Sean says.

"Yeah, sometimes I can't stand it."

Sean has on a white oxford shirt, with a black t-shirt underneath, a pair of jeans with a cool belt. It's black leather with a solid round silver fastener. His hair hangs, as it always does, over his oak-colored eyes.

"You look great tonight," he says, "I mean, you look great every day, but tonight, too." He looks out the window, back at me, and out the window again. I can't tell, but I think he's nervous.

"Thanks. I like your belt."

"My belt?" He cranes his neck like a swan aiming for sleep, "Oh yeah, I like this belt, too."

Sean's brother keeps looking in the rearview mirror, checking up on us. "For God's sake, Sean," he eventually says, "at least hold her hand." In the mirror I see him wink, wink at me.

"Shut up." Sean takes my hand, moves closer to me. "That's Patrick. He's always telling me what to do."

"Hi, Patrick," I say, not looking at him directly, but at his face in the rearview.

"Don't believe everything Sean tells you. He's the real boss in our household." Patrick glances back and forth between the road and the mirror; he settles on looking down the road.

Sean's hands are soft like Dad's; soft like the carpet in Samantha's office. I try to relax, even though my heart flutters in my chest. Breathe, one, two, three, I remind myself.

"How's your leg?" Sean asks.

"It still hurts every now and then, but nowhere near as bad as it did."

"That's good." We both look away, take in the road ahead for a moment.

"I saw you running the other day. You looked great." My face gets hot when I say this. Oops, I said too much. Sean blushes.

"I love to run," he says. "Isn't it great how you get in this rhythm and everything else just falls away?" He's turned toward me and is holding my hand in both of his. His palms are wet. "I get this feeling I can run forever. Some days I just want to try, to keep going."

"I know what you mean. I love the *shh, shh, shh* sound of running. I don't know if it is my heart or in my ears, but I love that sound." I move in toward Sean so I can see his face in the pulse of streetlights.

"Yeah! Exactly! Me, too!" Sean lets go of my hand. He shifts his arm up and around my shoulder. With the tentative nature of his movement, he seems to be asking my permission with every passing second. I don't stop him.

We sit like that for several moments, wrapped in a sweet silence.

"Hey," Sean loosens his arm around my shoulder and turns toward me slightly, "are you crying?"

"No. Not really." Tears have formed and maybe even fallen. I just can't admit I'm crying. "I wish I could run." Sean turns forward again and hugs me close. I rest my hand on his chest, near his heart.

"I don't know what I'd do if I had to give up running for a few months. This must be so tough for you."

"It would be even harder for you; you've been running a long time. I remember you running in grammar school!" We both laugh. "I only started running a few weeks ago—it's just that I liked it. A lot. I didn't know that

I would." I snuggle into the crook of Sean's arm. I'm not exactly comfortable, yet I don't want to move. I'm sad, and yet feel warm and happy inside.

"How long before you can run again?" Sean reaches over with his right hand and pushes a few strands of hair back from my face.

"The doctor says I'll be on crutches for another month. Then I'll have to jog in the pool before I run on the track."

Shadows and light keep painting Sean's profile. No one says a word.

Finally Sean offers, "It's a long time to be on crutches, but you'll get through it. We'll get through it."

My ears get hot at the soothing sound of Sean's support. On those days when I am miserable, this is a moment I will want to remember.

"Sean?"

"Yeah?"

"You know that I'm seeing a therapist, right?" I drop my hand from his chest, but don't know where to put it; he takes it into his own.

"Yeah."

"Do you think it's weird?"

"Heck no, it's kind of cool. I wish I could go." He pulls me closer. "My dad bugs me and I get really mad. I'm not nice." He lets go of my hand to clench and unclench his fist. "The other day I wanted to punch Kevin."

I breathe in and out, not sure what to say. "Sometimes, I'm not nice, too." The car passes over a stretch of grooved road. The *thwat, thwat, thwat* rises through the floorboard.

"I hate it when I get mad." He brushes my hair back on the other side now. "Especially when it's over nothing."

"Yeah. Therapy helps. I'm glad I see Samantha, but I don't want people to think I'm weird."

We drive on listening to the pulse of the road. My breathing synchronizes with Sean's—slow and regular.

"I'm going to see my mother on Monday." Why do I keep speaking? I wish I would shut up already.

Sean holds me and waits. He doesn't say a word. He's so quiet I can hear his heartbeat, his breath, his body circulating oxygenated blood.

"Are you nervous?" He asks after a pause, a stride.

"Yeah. I am." The skin tingles around my bones. I can't tell if it's because Sean's arm around my shoulder makes me feel electrified, or if it's because I'm nervous about Monday. It's strange how nerves and excitement feel the same.

"Sean, I don't think Patrick knows where the movie theater is. We've been driving a long time." I've noticed that Patrick still checks on us in the rearview, although with less frequency.

"He likes to drive. He said if we wanted, he'd take the long way to the theater."

"It would be okay with me if we never got there." I

bite my lip so as to not say too much about how much I like this—just driving around.

"I owe my brother one," Patrick pipes in, "so if you want to skip the movie and see the sights of Centerville instead, I can keep driving."

"Is that okay with you? If we just drive?" Sean asks tilting his head so we can see each other.

"Sure. This is nice." I don't mean to, but I move my hand up and down Sean's side. The movement is slight, but more than I intended.

"I like it too." Sean strokes my shoulder.

Patrick heads out toward the main road, the road that will take you around, through and out of town—wherever you want to go. He no longer checks up on us in the rearview mirror.

I watch the lights play across the back of the front seat, across Sean's long legs, across his graceful chest and against his pink lips, strong nose, brown eyes. I practice closing my eyes and recalling every angle of his face.

Without saying a word Sean lifts my chin. He doesn't do anything else, just that. However, I respond by lifting my face from his fingers and kissing his quiet open mouth. He tastes sweet like strawberry jam. I kiss him again.

Breathe, one, two, three. I feel woozy and warm and good from head to toes. I'd be content to drive and drive and drive—only stopping when we can't drive, or run, or walk another step. This is the first time in weeks that I've forgotten about everything else except Sean and the wonderful *shh, shh, shh* sound of running and driving.

CHAPTER 15

I wake to the sound of Dad's cheery voice. "Hey, kiddo, wake up. Rise 'n shine!" He knocks on the door, then pokes his head into my room. "Margie called. She's on her way over. She wants to hear all about the movie you—ahem—saw last night."

"Dad!" I grab the pillow out from under my head and toss it at the door. Last night, when I came home and Dad asked me how the movie was, I said "Okay." He said, "Really? It was 'Okay'?" I knew then and there he could tell it was a fib. Do all 911 operators have this special gift? Can they all hear things that are never said?

"When she arrives, I'll send Margie in, but then the two of you should come to the table for breakfast. So up and at 'em." He pulls his head back and closes the door. I can hear him singing some Broadway tune as he heads back to the kitchen.

"Uggh," I roll on my side, wishing for a few more minutes of sleep, knowing that I have to get up. My leg is killing me again. With every dull throb I'm reminded of the upcoming visit with Mom.

"Tell me! Tell me!" Margie knocks, rushes, bubbles into my room. Just my luck, Dad and Margie are both happy early risers.

"More sleep." I haven't gotten very far in my attempt to wake, shower, and dress.

"Don't pull that on me, McKane." Margie nudges my shoulder, literally trying to shake me out of my morning stupor. "Now come on, spill."

The thing is, I can't talk about last night without getting that swirly, dreamy feeling—and being embarrassed. I'm not sure why. It wasn't THAT big of a deal, a few kisses.

"It was fun. We had fun." I prop myself up against the headboard. My pillow is still over by the door where it landed after I threw it at Dad.

"Describe this fun you're talking about." Margie gives me an "I'm serious" look.

"You know, we talked. We talked about running. That's all." I'm doing my best. But Margie's eyes scrunch together in the facial equivalent of a question mark.

"I thought you were going to the movies."

"We were." I shake my head a couple of times. "We were, we just didn't." I can't help myself; I start to smile.

"Oh my gosh," Margie whispers. "You didn't go to the movies?"

"It's okay, Dad knows. I don't know how but he knows."

"Well? What did you do?" Margie bounces the bed in her excitement. My leg complains; it thinks of Monday. I hold my hand up to settle Margie. "Sorry. Sorry," she says, as she attempts to stop the runaway jumps.

"Sean has an older brother, Patrick, who likes to drive. So he drove us around town, down by the river, out toward the park." I wish I had my pillow to cover my face. I feel that burn coming on. "Like I said, 'It was fun.'"

"Did you hold hands?"

I nod.

"Did he put his arm around you?"

I nod.

"Andrea! Did he kiss you?"

I look down toward my navel and nod my head several times. I'm hoping my hair conceals what I'm sure is my beet-red face.

"Oh my God, you didn't do anything else, did you?" Margie rolls onto her knees. She bounces without moving the bed.

I jerk up, my eyes widen and I shake my head in a strong "No!"

"Sorry, but I want details. I want to know everything." Margie scoots up beside me on the bed so we are both leaning our backs against the headboard. All of a sudden my room looks overly white, pink, and light blue, like I'm sleeping in a crib.

"We had a good time. We talked and drove around." I nudge my shoulder into Margie's. She nudges back.

"Breakfast!" Dad calls from the kitchen.

"Okay, I'll give you a reprieve for now. But sooner or later I want details."

"Geez, you sound like a drill sergeant."

"That's me. Now get up. Your dad said he was making a super-delicious extravaganza breakfast." Margie picks Pedro up off of my desk, brushes his ears, brushes her nose against his. "Matthew doesn't even know I exist." She jabs Pedro back on the stack of papers cluttering the desktop. "Remember, Pedro, it's you and me at the prom."

"Stop it." I throw back the covers and swing my legs over the side of the bed. It hurts. Morning is the worst. My leg doesn't like being without its cast all night. Breathe in, one, two, three. Breathe out. "We had a good time at Dino's." I inch closer to the edge of the bed. "Matthew likes you tons. He's just shy. Really shy."

"Not like Sean." Margie makes kissing noises.

"Hey, hey." I push myself up onto one foot and hop over to my dresser. Each step sends a shock of fire up my back. "This is the no-teasing zone." I get my clothes together. Dad calls us from the kitchen. "Go let Dad amuse you with his famous flapjack tricks."

I use the shirt in my hand to shoo-shoo Margie out of my room.

Dressing—one of those things that used to be relatively easy and is now complicated by hopping and sitting and a big boot. I can't pull pants over my good leg if I'm standing on it, and I can't pull them over my butt if I'm sitting on it. Getting dressed is complicated.

"There you are." Dad holds a plate of pancakes and sausages swimming in sweet maple syrup.

"Wait for me." I swing over to the dining table.

"Your dad won't tell me the secret to making perfectly round pancakes. Look—these are all—" Margie tilts her plate so I can see her round, round stack of flapjacks, "—perfectly round."

"I know. He's weird that way." I'm so hungry I'm almost eating before I settle in my seat.

"Orange juice? Tea? Anything to drink?" My dad asks.

"I'd like a cup of coffee," I say, shoveling food into my mouth.

"Oh, how I wish you had never started drinking coffee." Dad turns toward the kitchen, "Margie, anything for you?"

"No thanks, Mr. McKane. I'm good."

Dad goes into the kitchen. I can hear him getting a cup, sugar, milk. I can smell the coffee. How I love that smell.

"Here you go." He sets a cup on the table in front of me and takes a seat for himself. For a few minutes the only sound is the clicks of our forks against our plates.

"Dad?" I lay my fork in a pool of syrup on my plate. "Can we talk about Mom? About Monday?" I'm as surprised by my questions as I imagine Dad and Margie are. This morning has been almost perfect; perfect except for this one, insistent worry. My thoughts must be making up for all the forgetting I did last night.

"Uhh, sure. Now?" Dad asks. He looks at me, then Margie.

"Yeah, Margie's okay. Right?" I hoist my coffee mug in Margie's direction. It is as though some other person is in control. I have no idea what I'll say or do next.

"Sure. I'm okay," Margie says. She squints her eyes. I don't think she believes what she sees.

I swallow deeply; my heart rises in my throat. "I just want to know—" I return my cup to the safety of the table, "Do I have to go?"

Dad flips a butter knife, a clean knife, over and over on the table. Setting it so the blade of the knife faces left, then right, then left again.

I don't say anything, but listen.

"Not if you don't want to." He pushes the knife away and looks at me. "Do you want to skip it?"

I look at Dad, then down at my plate. "I'm not sure." Mostly, I want to have a choice, to be able to say yes or no.

Margie eats her pancakes and watches Dad, then me, as though she were watching a tennis match. Her eyes go left, right, left.

Dad drums his fingers the way Samantha does when she is thinking. He leans toward me, "I think it would be good for you to see her." He puts his hand over mine. "But if you don't want to—" He squeezes then lets go. "Maybe later would be better." He leans back.

"If I did go, would you come into the room with me?" I flip my fork over once, then twice, imitating Dad. I smell summer when the syrup is disturbed.

"Absolutely. If that's what you want, I'll be there." Dad sits taller.

I drink my coffee. Breathe.

"Okay." I bite my bottom lip a few times—bad habit that I've developed out of nowhere. "I'll go."

Dad waits. Margie waits. I have to remember to take a breath.

"Okay," Dad says.

"Okay," I say again, nodding my head.

I look at Margie, she mouths, "It'll be okay." She gives me a quiet thumbs up.

I'm not so hungry anymore, and push away my plate. Dad and Margie, too, have stopped eating.

"Thanks, Dad." I take another sip of coffee. "Breakfast was great."

"You make the best pancakes." Margie gets up, collects her plate, Dad's, and mine. It's impossible to clear the table while using crutches. I know because I tried. Once.

"It was my pleasure. My pleasure." Dad pats his belly to show his satisfaction.

I breathe in the rich, dark, roast of bean, the bitter of my coffee, which hovers at the edge of my cup. At first I didn't like the smell of coffee, and now it's my favorite part. Maybe, just maybe, Monday will be like that.

Chapter 16

"Damn it!" A waterfall of books and papers escapes my locker as I open it. What doesn't fall on its own, I yank out.

At the end of last period, I'd seen Kevin in the hallway and he thrust his hips at me. We were passing each other and for no reason he has to be a jerk. I wish he would find someone else to harass besides Matthew, Sean, and me. I probably shouldn't have called him slug sputum.

"Damn it!" I slam the metal door shut. The bang is loud and empty.

"Take it easy!" Margie stoops to pick up my debris. It's the end of the day, and Margie and I are the only two who haven't gone home or off to band, or track, or student council, or something.

"*You* take it easy!" I say much too loudly, hopping around. "Forget it. Leave it." I lean my crutches against the lockers, but they fall over in a loud clackety clatter. I bend over, my broken leg sticking out—I'm trying to get to the floor without killing myself.

"Damn it, Margie, I said forget it!" I snatch my papers from Margie's hand. She stares at me, her mouth all "Oh my God!"-looking.

"This is really the way you want to act? Like a total jerk?" Margie stands, puts her hands on her hips. She looks just like her mother does when she's yelling at her to clean her room.

"If it wasn't, I wouldn't be acting this way." My leg sends spears of pain up through my back and neck. It's as though the papers and things from the locker are floating in a pool of water. The closer I get, the quicker they bob away.

"Stop being a jerk. Just because you're going to see your mother—" Margie isn't helping me, she just watches. I'm boiling like a stormy sky.

"I told you to FORGET IT. LEAVE ME ALONE!"

Margie stares, shakes her head.

"I'd like to leave you alone right now. Believe me." Margie kneels at the far edge of the widening spill. "Sometimes, you are an idiot."

I'm so tired. I give up my awkward crouch and my feeble attempts at collecting papers and just sit. My legs extend out in front of me, one gigantic like a breakwater, the other narrow like a mound of sand. I'm the biggest, craggiest rock.

I stretch out to reach the things that I can reach. Margie is containing the toxic spread, making stacks of paper. It's barely November—how did I collect so much stuff so fast?

"Andrea?" Margie loses the rose in her cheeks. She touches the stone circle at her throat; it, too, has faded to gray.

I scoot my butt back against the locker bank; I'm paralyzed from the waist down. "Yeah?"

Lavender paper. Margie is holding out an envelope, it has the faint scent of lilac or lavender. My mother's drug-agitated scrawl runs from the middle to the edge of the page. The curve of the cursive is chunky, like Eddie Weasel's valentine heart.

It's too late, now, to say no. To tell Margie, "Don't find that letter. No matter what. Whatever you do." My heart races; I feel lightheaded.

I take the envelope from Margie's hand. My hands shake. Hers do, too.

"Is this the 'bad' letter?"

Nodding, I lower the letter to my lap. Margie abandons her round-up work and sits next to me.

"Do you want to read it?" Margie asks.

The letter, my hands, even my chest, all tremble as I open it. It's difficult to decipher, as it is a mess of shaky script, cross-outs, and food stains.

I return it to my lap for a moment. "Remember when Mom used to write me notes, in perfect penmanship, and put them in my lunch bag?" I'm not sure if I even knew Margie then. It was a long time ago.

"She did?" Margie asks.

"The i's were dotted, the t's crossed, every loop closed, and all the letters the same height. I loved her notes."

"What did they say?" Margie is still; her hands are quietly folded in her lap.

"She'd put them in my lunch bags, they'd say things like—*Don't doubt yourself! I love you, forever and always!* and *You are the sunshine in my rainy day.* I was the only kid in my class to get notes like that. It was cool." I'm picking at the corner of the envelope and the American flag stamp.

"You hadn't told me that. That *is* cool."

"I should tell you more of the good things Mom did. Not just the crazy stuff."

Margie nods. "We could just shove the letter back in the bottom of your locker or throw it away." She puts her hand on my quivering wrist.

"No. I think it's here on my lap for a reason. I'm supposed to read it again." With the speed of a turtle, a slow one at that, I lift the envelope flap.

I struggle to slide the note from it, because it sticks and pulls on both sides. The letter begins:

Dear Andrea,

I know that you think you are better than me—that I let you down and hurt you and you don't want anything to do with me.

Between the rattle of my hands and the quiver of her penmanship it feels like we're having an earthquake. Stop reading, stop reading, stop reading, is all I hear as I continue.

It is a shame, really. I worked so hard to teach you to be kind and to not judge others. Obviously, I did not work hard enough.

There are several cross-outs or smudges here. I can't tell what she had written.

Remember, my darling daughter, remember where you came from. It was from between my legs that you struggled your way into the world. I panted and heaved and cried out from the pain you caused me, and then you were born.

Breathe, breathe, breathe. Even my calming voice has lost its soothe.

You were covered in white mucus, a repulsive sight, but I loved you just the same.

Margie drops her hand from her open mouth. "I don't think you should read anymore. That's enough."

"You can't tell me what I can and cannot read!"

"I wasn't saying you couldn't read it." If hallways had weather, the black clouds would be forming tight knots and the lightning bolts would be striking like machine-gun fire. "I don't want to see you hurt." Margie fidgets with the bottom of her shirt.

"Well, don't look then." I'm on fire. I imagine smoke rising from the top of my head, that's how sizzly I feel. "Just leave me alone! GET OUT of here!" Surprising myself, I push Margie on the shoulder—not in a kidding way at all.

"Hey! Knock it off." Margie moves away from me.

"I mean it, Margie, go! Get out of here. Leave ME ALONE." With my good leg I kick at the neat stack of paper that Margie had collected for me earlier. My mess doubles in size. I notice the next line of my mother's letter:

You are just like me—always have been.

"McKane, you really piss me off sometimes." Margie is back on her feet. "Aargh! I want to kick something."

"Me too!" I yell back and strike the heel of my broken leg on the gray tiled floor. The ricochet of fire runs up through my leg and back so fast, I choke on bile before I even realize I'm in pain.

"That does it! I'm leaving you here in your pile of shit, but only because if I stay you'll do something so asinine I'll never forgive you." Margie grabs her backpack and starts down the hall.

"Good! Go! That's what I wanted!" I screech at her receding back.

When I was a young girl I had so many dreams and hopes. I wanted to fall in love, marry, and have children. I wanted to dance under the stars, and swim in all the oceans of the world. I had dreams just like you—but in the end all my dreams amounted to nothing more than a pile of shit.

Mom was right about this.

Just remember that, when you imagine what your future might be like. Life has a way of surprising you.

She was right about this, too.

I wish you'd write or visit. This hospital is hell. Everyone here is so busy talking to God and aliens; they just aren't interested in chatting, over a cup of tea, with a mere mortal. What am I talking about, we can't have tea anyway—someone might get burned. They treat us like children.

I'm coming, Mom. Today, in fact.

Hopefully, one of these days, all the cookies-and-cream nurses will leave me alone long enough that I'll be able to end my life. I'd like to give that to you for your birthday. You'll be the only girl to get her mother's suicide as a gift.

My teeth chatter like small thunderclaps between my ears.

Believe me, all your teenage friends will be envious as all get-out. No girl loves her mother—so you are boring and normal in this regard.

Breathe—one, two, three. I must remember to

breathe. I should have forgotten it, thrown it away. I should have listened to myself.

Love, Your crazy mother

I scrunch the letter, pull it apart, tear it one way, then tear it the other. I'm making confetti, a machine on hyper-drive. I tear and tear and tear, and throw the handful of sweet lilac breath toward the opposite wall. The purple snow meets a cold front and drops in clumps on my legs.

"Damn it! Damn it!"

I have to find Dad. He's probably waiting for me.

"Damn it!" I knock the confetti chunks onto the floor, onto a piece of paper. Scattered around is an English quiz, Algebra homework, my report on Skinner's Box. Sheets and remnants everywhere.

I grab a piece of paper and scootch, and grab a piece of paper, "Damn it! Damn it! Damn it!" I pick up my psych book and stack it onto the pile of collected school papers, books—and next to the pile of scrap—all that's left of my letter from Mom.

CHAPTER 17

Dad rushes over to me. "Andrea! Hey, kiddo, are you okay?"

I'm breathing hard; I feel like I just sprinted a quarter mile.

"What happened?" Dad is always working; always the voice of calm no matter how bad the accident.

"Nothing, Dad." I stand on one foot, hand my crutches to him, and remove my backpack.

"Now I know what they mean when they say, 'You look like you've seen a ghost.' That's just how you look." Dad slides the crutches into the back seat. He also takes my backpack, which I'm holding out in front of me.

"Can we just go?" I hop over to the passenger door of the stupid Datsun. Why doesn't my father have a bigger car, one that is easier for me to get into?

"Sure." Dad keeps extending his hands toward me, like he wants to help me get into the car. In the end, though, he's just pushing air around; there's no way he can make getting in the car any easier. "Where's Margie?" he asks. "I thought she was carrying your books." He closes the car door after I am finally situated.

"Margie's the ghost. She disappeared."

"Hmm—" Dad reaches into the back seat as he gets into the car. "I brought you something." He hands me Pedro. "He was worried about you."

Seeing Pedro, I feel that quivery sensation in my chest. I hug him to me and flatten his ears against his head the way I like to do.

Dad drives away from the school. We don't speak. I notice that he looks over at me five or ten times more often than he usually does.

"I'm not going anywhere." I look out the window. Pine trees rise up in sharp points, piercing the sky. It is a gray day, damp and cool. At least it isn't raining.

"Right." He drives on, looks over at me, back at the road, over at me. "Are you nervous?"

"Well, you're freaking me out a little. Why do you keep looking at me?" I point Pedro's pink nose to the window so he, too, can see the spires of green.

"It scared me a little, how pale you were when you came out of school. I'm looking to see if your color is returning."

"Is it?" I stare straight ahead.

"Maybe a little—" Dad turns, brushes my hair back.

"—For God's sake watch the road!" I yell. Dad jerks his head forward, pumps the brake. The car jolts.

We both take rapid, sharp breaths, in one, out one, in one, out one.

"That did it, your color has returned. In fact, now

you're red as a beet." He moves his head back and forth so fast I'm afraid he's going to sprain his neck.

"Yeah, thanks." I twist away from him. Every look feels like a hand on my face.

We drive on. The trees thicken, the buildings thin. I wonder why the hospital is so far out of town. Are the patients kept away from the rest of us, or are the rest of us kept away from them?

"We're almost there." Again, Dad checks on me, the road, me, the road. I drop my shoulder barrier.

"Yep." A few miles back I started to nibble at my lower lip.

"You still want me to go in with you?"

"No, that's okay." I shock myself with this answer. The closer I get to the hospital the more alone I feel; the more alone I want to be.

"You sure?" Dad has a tight grip on the wheel. "Because I'm happy to."

"I know." Pedro sits on my lap looking up at me. I flatten his ears then lift them up then flatten them again. "Dad? When did Mom get sick?"

Dad runs a hand over his head.

"I mean—the time she made cookies and put some on a plate for the birds. We drank tea and watched the chickadees. Was she sick then? Or did it all go bad later?" Pedro's ears stand straight up as though he's just seen a bear, or thinks he has. I swear his eyes widen.

"I don't know." Dad brushes up the short hairs at the nape of his neck a couple of times. "When I married her, she was radiant and beautiful. She was so happy when she had you. We were all happy then."

"Was she really? Happy, I mean, when she had me?"

"Andrea," Dad looks over at me, then steers the car onto the shoulder of the road. He puts on the hazard lights and turns to me in his seat. One arm on the wheel, the other braced against the seat back, "She was. She loved you so much." He tilts his head trying to look underneath the long strands of hair that I've used to create a curtain between him and me.

"What happened then?" My voice rattles in my throat. I'm running out of spit.

"Kiddo, look at me." He reaches over and pulls my hair back. "She got sick. I don't know why. It just happens."

"Can anyone get sick?" I rub Pedro's fur against my face, hoping he'll mop up the tears that are running down my cheeks.

"Schizophrenia isn't like the flu." Dad looks down at the floorboards for a second. "It's not contagious or anything."

I freeze for a beat when Dad says schizophrenia. We don't say it very often.

I lift and smoosh Pedro's ears. Dad turns back in his seat and reaches for the ignition.

"Wait—"

Dad doesn't turn the key but he doesn't look at me either.

I love him for that.

"What about me? Am I sick? Is that why I'm seeing Samantha?"

"Oh, Andrea," Dad takes a long breath in. "No, you're not sick. And that is definitely not, I repeat, that is *not* why you're seeing Samantha." Dad runs both hands over his head, each one taking a side. I think he wants to look at me, and is holding his head forward so he doesn't. "Your mother's been so hard on you. I just wanted you to have support. That's all."

I'm using Pedro like a handkerchief now; his ears wash the wet from my face.

"There are so many things I don't understand about your mother's illness. Why she's so mean, for example." His voice dips. "Listen, Andrea, if you don't want to go to therapy you don't have to." Dad hugs the steering wheel in both arms.

"No. I want to." We are stopped on a road that's nowhere. No buildings, no people, no other cars. Pine trees only and the faintest hint, just ahead, of a place to turn.

"I'm glad," Dad says, "that therapy is helping."

Dad turns the key in the ignition, the engine squawks to life. "Are you ready?"

Pedro nods, I nod, then Dad does, too. "Okay."

He puts his seatbelt back on, checks over his shoulder, and pulls back out onto the road. We don't travel but another 400 yards or so, when we turn off the main road to Brookmoor Psychiatric Hospital.

We pass through the stand of trees at the edge of the road, through the bushes that border the yard, and down the path that curves through the lawn. The grass, though yellow and dead, has been recently cut.

"Look, Pedro," I whisper into his ear as we both press our noses to the window, "it's a big white house with lots and lots of windows." Pedro wipes his damp cheek against mine and we promise each other everything will be okay.

CHAPTER 18

"You must be Andrea." The nurse extends her hand to shake, which I do, awkwardly because of the crutches. "I'm Vivian." She points to the name tag on her pink nurse's coat.

"Hello."

"Hello, Mr. McKane. It's nice to see you again." Vivian shakes Dad's hand as well. He's visited Mom a few times, so some of the nurses know him. "Mrs. McKane had a difficult time last night. She's in her room resting." She motions for us to follow her as she makes her way down the hall. "Take that out of your mouth, George," she calls, as we pass the lounge and she sees a patient with a towel hanging from his mouth.

"Ta' tha' ou' o' 'ur 'out'?" He waves his arms and stands on one leg, bends the other, a crane spreading his wings. I wonder if he's making fun of me as I do a one-legged walk myself.

"George, behave. Take the towel out of your mouth. Now!"

He just grins, a blue terry cloth tongue hanging from his teeth, arms open, and his body wavering on one leg.

"Her room is right here." Vivian points toward an open door, the lights dim inside. "She's been given a sedative, so she's groggy."

Vivian takes a step closer to me. "Also, she's been restrained—for her own safety."

Even though Vivian is talking to me, I quickly look at Dad. This is the first time I'm glad I have crutches; it's good to have something to lean on.

"You okay, kiddo?" Dad and Vivian both wait, I'm not sure for what.

"Can she hear us out here?" I whisper.

"Probably not." Vivian waves her hand at George who is galloping down the hallway with the towel still hanging out of his mouth. "George! Back to the Day Room."

"Oh nu's. 'ac' 'o 'he 'ay room," George mumbles as he stops his galumphing walk, drops his shoulders and walks to the lounge area.

"Will Mom know me?" I keep looking over my shoulder toward the Day Room. I wonder if George has difficult nights, too.

"I think she'll recognize you—her speech may be slurred and she may not be able to stay awake for very long."

"Great." I take a couple of strides forward. "Well, I'll just go in then." Dad takes a deep breath; I can hear him.

"I'll be right out here," he says.

"Thanks, Dad."

I knock on the open door. There is light in the room, although it has been dimmed. It comes from those lights that point upward and run along the wall near the ceiling. They're night-lights for adults.

"Mom?" Her room is a double. However, the other bed has been stripped. I don't think anyone is sleeping in it. Mom lies on her back; she opens her eyes when I enter.

"You came," she says looking nowhere but up. I peek at the ceiling myself, to see if there's something interesting up there. There isn't.

"How are you?" My voice breaks a little. Damn, I don't want my words to flutter.

"That's funny." Mom closes her eyes.

I take a few more swings to get near her bed, and then have to hop around to get to the chair. I tug, tug at the chair, try to move it close to the bed. Finally I realize it's attached to the floor. What a dummy. "I can't move the chair, Mom. It's stuck."

"It's secured to insure the safety of the patients. I am much safer now that that chair will not be moving about, sneaking up behind me while I'm in the shower, or playing checkers in the Day Room. I am so safe." Her voice is monotone. It gives me the shivers; it's creepy.

"Do you need anything?" I don't have a clue what to say.

"Can you remove these?" She jerks both her wrists; the leather straps stop them cold. She keeps jerking.

"Mom. Don't." My voice rises and squeaks a little. Thank goodness, Mom stops pulling and drops her hands by her sides again. For the first time she drops her head to the side so she can see me.

"I heard your leg is broken."

"Yep." I lift my elephant foot so she can see it better.

"That sucks," she says. It's interesting how uncomfortable that makes me.

"It isn't that bad."

There is a silence that has been creeping around and now it jumps on the bed between us. Nothing is said. I'm not sure if I should leave or not, when my mother speaks again. "I understand you like to run." She returns to the ceiling and closes her eyes.

"I did." Nerves bubble up in excited speech. "It was Margie's idea, and I thought she was—" I can't say the word. "Then I really liked it. I did, until I broke my leg. I didn't get to be on the track team for very long, but I loved to run. I didn't know I would, but I really did." I'm breathing hard, like I just sprinted a quarter mile. "Sorry. I mean, I do. I do like to run."

"This just gets funnier and funnier." My mother says in her deadpan. She repeatedly licks her lips.

"Do you want something to drink?" I ask.

"A scotch and soda would be ever so nice." She smiles, sort of. Her tongue pushes at her top lip as though the smile doesn't taste good. I'm not sure what to say in response so I look at the floor.

"Is there a boy?" Mom asks. I look around, trying to convince myself that she's asking about someone in the room. For some reason, I don't want to answer the question.

"I like a boy, if that's what you mean." The room begins to feel like a sauna.

"At least you're not a les-bi-an." She accentuates and draws out the word.

"Mom!"

The silence circles a few times. I want to go home.

"I'm sorry. Tell me about the boy." The fingers of her right hand type out letters on the bedspread. She doesn't seem to notice.

"His name is Sean." Agitation bubbles, again, in my throat. "He runs track, too."

"Is he smart?" Her left hand now joins in the typing. I push myself up from the chair. She hasn't opened her eyes for the last ten minutes or so.

"Yes, Mom, he's smart." I lean over and put my hand over hers. "I'm going to go now, it was good—"

Mom slides her hand out from under mine and grabs my wrist. It is like a magic trick, a sleight of hand. Her eyes pop open and she pulls herself up. Instinctively, I retreat. Everything is happening faster than I can run.

"—Beware the smart ones." Her face is waxy and her eyes glow.

"Mom, let go." I yank harder. Mom releases me, so I fall backwards with my crutches criss-crossing in front of me.

"Hah. You always were a klutz." Mom barks a laugh and disappears behind her eyes. "You're just like your mother. Mark my words, you and me, we're the same." Her fingers continue to press on invisible keys.

My leg is banging with pain. I didn't actually fall but I must have put weight on my broken leg.

"Andrea?" Dad is at the door. "Are you okay?"

I take several long silent strides to get out of the room. Mom has returned to her corpselike sleep. Dad scratches the back of his head, in a movement that looks like he's asking, "What the hell is going on?"

"Andrea?" Dad follows me.

I whomp, whomp, whomp down the hall. Dad has to quicken his walk to catch up with me. I want to stay ahead of him so he won't see me crying. I can't talk right now.

George startles me by taking a couple of hops in my direction. I didn't see him standing around the corner. His arms are outstretched and he's as big as a Grizzly. "Ru'! Ru'!" he yells through his terry cloth tongue. "Ru'!"

I wish I could, I wish I could.

Chapter 19

"So, Andrea, how was your visit with your mom?" Samantha's hair is messed up, and she looks tired and bored.

"You look terrible," I say. My arms are crossed, and the only thing that interests me is seeing how far I can bury my hand in the crook of my elbow. I wish I hadn't agreed to this "after-visit" session.

Samantha sits, taps her fingers, watches me.

"Why do you do that?" I ask, without looking up.

"Do what?" she asks.

"Just sit there." If I tug my left elbow with my right hand, then my left hand almost disappears below my arm.

"Andrea, look at me." Samantha's voice is flat and solid.

"I'm not looking at you. You look terrible, just like I said." If I squeeze my forearms together I can almost see my hand emerging from my upper arm.

"Apparently your visit with your mom didn't go very well." She quietly taps her fingers, just like my mother. What is it with these women and their finger typing?

"Shows how much you know. It was fine." Even the rug is ugly today. "She didn't do anything but lay there. She was even tied to the bed." I laugh.

Samantha sits, breathes, waits.

"Cut it out, will you?" I uncross my arms, sit forward on the couch. If she types the arm of her chair one more time I'll scream.

"Cut what out, Andrea?" Samantha is using that even tone on purpose, I bet. She's trying to bug me.

"You know—that tap, tap, tap bullshit!" I hit the arm of the couch several times.

"I can see that you are upset, and I hear that you're angry." Samantha leans forward, rests her elbows on her knees the way she always does. "Can you tell me what happened? How was it seeing your mom?"

"Do you know what is stupid?" I lean forward and rest my elbows on my knees just like Samantha. She sits back. I sit back. I imitate her every move. "I'm serious, do you know what's stupid?" I spit the words out as if they are sharp-pointed bullets.

"No, I don't." Samantha shakes her head. "Can you tell me?"

I grab a throw pillow and hug it to my chest. It isn't anywhere near as easy to cross my arms around the pillow. Mostly, I am grabbing my wrists.

I swing my head back and forth, copying Samantha.

"Andrea, please—this acting out isn't beneficial to

you." She is trying to make eye contact with me, I can tell, even though I'm not looking anywhere except at the criss-cross of my arms.

"Forget it, you don't have to answer me. I was just asking." I grab my wrists then pull them apart, then grab them again and pull them apart. The tearing feels strange. "I shouldn't be here. It was stupid to come. It's stupid to keep up this blah-blah-blah."

Samantha leans forward in her chair, tilts her head in a question, and looks at me, and looks at me for one breath, then two.

"It's stupid," I say again, no longer sure what I'm saying or why.

"Are you telling me that you would like to end this session, and that you'd rather not talk about the visit with your mom?"

No. I stop pulling at my hands. *No.* Every leaf stops rustling, every car stops grumbling, and the furnace does-n't blow or hiss—all sounds go quiet. *No.* Even my breath is silent.

"Breathe, Andrea—breathe in, one, two, three and out, one, two, three."

"Are you saying I need to go? What do I do? Just leave? Sit in the waiting room?" It is as though my legs and arms have been strapped to the couch. I can't move.

"No, you don't have to leave. In fact, I hope you don't. I'm just asking you to talk to me. It's important that we talk about your visit with your mother." Samantha leans forward again, her fingertips pressed together. "It's possible that your mother will be going home in a few weeks. I want to help you prepare."

Inadvertently, I jerk my head like I have water in my ears. I did not just hear what I heard. I couldn't have.

"Why? How?" My good foot tap, tap, taps. My leg bounces. My bad leg hurts, hurts, hurts in rhythmic spikes. "I'm not ready!" Breathe—one, two, three.

"I know. Unfortunately, though, without criminal charges, your mom's stay at the hospital has been, essentially, voluntary. She has expressed the desire to return home. Legally, if she is well enough, no one can stop her from being discharged."

"But she's not well enough. She had a 'difficult' night the night before last. She's a mess." Even my bad foot is trying to agitate. "This is what's stupid!" I say pointing at Samantha. "This is STUPID!" My pointed finger joins the rest in a fist and smashes my leg, my broken leg.

"Andrea! Stop!" Samantha asserts in a loud, firm voice. Then softly, "We're all concerned for your safety. That's our highest concern."

"Bullshit!" I try to get up. It's too hot. "Bullshit! Bullshit! Bullshit!" The room is beginning to fall away in creamy swirls. "No one gives a shit about my safety." Every time I pick up a crutch, I drop it. I feel like I'm juggling crutches.

Samantha stands up. She stands in my way but she also reaches down and picks up the crutch that I just dropped for the fiftieth time. She hands it to me.

"I'm sorry, Andrea. I know this is scary."

"Scary? Scary?" I swing my crutches forward so fast Samantha steps back to avoid being hit. "You don't know scary." One long stride is all it takes to reach the door.

"Andrea, it's understandable that you want to leave. But, as I said, I hope you decide to stay. There's a lot we need to talk about."

I can't turn the doorknob. I pull at it, but it won't open. "Samantha! Just let me out!" I plead, rattling the knob. "Please! Please, let me go!"

Samantha approaches, she moves slowly. Standing behind me she says, "Andrea, I'll let you out if you want. However, can you stay for a few minutes more? How about if you stay for ten more minutes? If you still want to leave after that, then no problem."

I slap the door with the flat of my hand. "Let me out. Please, please."

"Andrea?"

I turn and slide to the floor; my broken leg juts into the room like a wide pipe. The crutches are like shotguns, one extended from each hip. I hug my other leg and pull it close. Samantha keeps her distance but also sits on the floor.

"I'm not ready. Why doesn't anyone understand? I'm not ready." My face is soaked. I'm drenched in sweat.

"Tell me."

Burying my face in the crook of my arm, on top of my knee, I feel squeezed into a tight dark spot. I don't ever want to lift my head.

"She's going to kill me," I talk to the blackness.

"Is that what she said?"

Maybe they're wrong about my leg. Maybe it's okay, and if I take off this stupid boot I'll be able to walk, and run and run and run, without any problem.

"Andrea? Where are you?" Lifting my head I see Samantha's face, my mother's face, the face of a monster. It's large and blubbery; it doesn't hold a shape. "Andrea?" Samantha jumps up and gets a blanket from her closet. She wraps it around my shoulders. I didn't realize but my teeth are chattering. "Andrea! Andrea! Look at me. Tell me what you see."

I look at Samantha. "I—" Tears jog down my cheeks. "I—" My chin quivers. "I—"

"Andrea, keep looking at me. Tell me what you see."

"I thought you were my—" I close the blanket under my chin. "I thought you were my—" I change from hot to cold and back to hot. "My mother." The room is heating up. "But you're not. You're Samantha."

"That's right." Samantha offers a small smile. "And I'm here to help you."

I must be crazy. I feel sick to my stomach. I'm on the floor of my therapist's office, and want, more than anything else, to lie down.

"I hurt," is all I can say.

"Tell me about the hurt."

Samantha and I breathe together.

I don't hear it, as much as I feel it rising from my chest—*shh, shh, shh* is the whisper of my heart.

Samantha waits.

"Mom seemed sick, really sick." I swallow a couple of times. I don't want to spit on Samantha's carpet. "How can they let her leave?" My chin rests on my knee—I like the pressure on my jaw when I speak. It makes me want to go "wah, wah, wah" and create a buzzing in my ears.

"In order to hospitalize a person against her will, she must be committed by a court. If you and your father want to pursue a legal commitment, I recommend talking to a lawyer. One with experience in this area." Samantha is looking under my hair, trying to make eye contact. "I won't lie to you. It's very difficult to have someone involuntarily committed, especially if they show positive regulation when properly medicated."

"That's 'blah-blah' talk for I don't have a chance." I pick at the square of the rug near my good foot.

"I'll support you any way I can. One way, is to prepare you for your mother's possible return."

There's a deep inhale—I think both Samantha and I breathe in at the same time. I'm riding a rollercoaster. I feel scared, then things quiet, then I'm scared again. Just the mention of my mother sends me screaming down the long, high drop of the ride.

"She's too sick. I'm telling you, she's too sick." I shake my head no.

"Can you tell me why you say she's too sick?"

I continue shaking my head no. I continue picking at the rug. "She's going to kill me."

"Tell me why you say that."

I shake, shake, shake. First I'm shaking my head, then my shoulders, then my legs and hands. It is as though I could vibrate into a million pieces.

"Can you draw? Not speak, but draw what you're feeling?"

I don't nod yes, but I stop my insistent no. Samantha gets up again and pulls a pad of paper from her closet, and some pens. Her closet is like a magician's hat; she's always surprising me with what's inside.

"Just take a pen and start drawing. Draw anything you want."

I take the blue pen out of the package. It is a deep, dark blue. My line squeaks along the page at first. I don't know what I'm drawing but it begins big and round with zigzags across the top, that turn into wild hair; I add eyes that have blue rivers of blood filling the whites. The head is huge in relation to the body and the legs are smaller yet. A large knife, the size of the whole torso of the figure, stands upright next to the head. Blue blood washes across the knife and spreads out like a lake below the feet of the figurine. I add a few jagged teeth, then cap the pen and place it on the paper.

"Very good," says Samantha. "Very good." She picks up the paper and moves it so we can both see it.

"What can you tell me about the knife?"

"It's big." I rock back and forth on my one bent leg.

"It *is* big. Did your mother use a knife the night the police came?"

"It's big." I repeat, rocking faster, shutting my eyes.

"Stay with me. Try to keep your eyes open and focused on me."

I open my eyes. Things look familiar. That's good.

"I feel sick."

"Try, Andrea. Try to talk about the knife."

"There's blue blood," I say, pointing my nose toward the picture.

"Whose blood is that?"

I shrug my shoulders. "All of ours."

Samantha picks up the drawing and brings it closer to me. "Where are you in this picture?"

I shake my head.

Samantha waits.

"Put 'you' in the picture. I want to know where you are."

With a shaky hand I pick up a black pen. I'm moving so slowly that it's creepy, even to me. In the bottom right-hand corner of the picture, I draw a tiny keyhole in a small box. The keyhole has a pupil and iris filling in the center. The tip of the pen is so thick, though, that I'm not sure anyone can tell what I've drawn.

Samantha gets up from her spot on the floor and peers over my shoulder, "Is that a keyhole? Is that your eye?"

I nod. Samantha can see things in a blob of ink. She can see things that aren't exactly there. Like me.

"Okay, now draw a protective wall between the 'you' in the box and the knife."

I continue to tremble, but do as Samantha asks. The line is thin and wavery at first, but then I scribble and scribble and scribble, until it is a thick, thick line; its ends run off the edges of the paper. Finishing, I lay the pen down and bury my head by my knee and under my arm once again. I'm crying and breathing hard, and I don't understand why.

"Great work, Andrea. Great work." Samantha gets up, disappears into her closet and emerges with something in her hand. "Here's another medallion for your box. You certainly have earned this today." She hands me a round piece of shiny metal. Thankfully, she puts a box of Kleenex near my leg as well. With tears running down my cheeks and my nose running, I'm a mess.

Before taking the medal, I take a tissue, then the round piece of metal. The word *Courageous* is printed on the front.

"Courageous," I say aloud.

"That's right. You, Andrea McKane, are a courageous young woman. I am proud to work with you."

In some ways it was easier, earlier in the session,

when Samantha looked awful. I didn't like her then. Now, her eyes are gentle, and sitting here with her makes me so sad. I wish she could hold me and brush my hair out of my face, and reassure me that everything is going to be all right, the way my mom used to. Before.

CHAPTER 20

There's crying. It's coming from out on the water. It sounds like a small girl. She's whimpering. The sky is swirling purple, blue, and gray. It looks like a bruise that's come alive. I'm standing on the shore, searching the water.

I see her. She's visible, then disappears below the surface, as though she's being tugged from below.

"Hold on!" I scream, although she has nothing to grasp. "I'm coming! Hold on!" I back up a step or two to increase my momentum. It's stupid; after all I'm not going to take flight. I start to run. I run into the water, taking high awkward steps as I hurdle each incoming wave. "Hold on!" I yell again, through sputtering salt and a whipping wind.

I keep running. My legs churn. They are not broken, they never have been. The water meets me in the chest, the neck, my mouth, nose, eyes, and then covers my head. I keep running. Even though I'm now several feet below the surface, I can still hear the *shh, shh, shh* of my strides. I'm looking up toward the sun, searching for that girl.

Running is difficult in the deep. My legs stay back,

my chest lunges ahead. I look like I'm perpetually falling forward.

I think I see the legs of the girl. She drops down and up and down again. Her pink taffeta skirt opens like a poppy in springtime, then closes as she rises.

"I'm coming," I blurble. Large bubbles escape my mouth. Each contains a word.

As I swim to the surface and the girl, a black film approaches her from all sides. It is the shutter of a camera about to close. "No!" I silently bubble.

The black ring becomes a keyhole, and the girl is gone as I approach. I can't reach the water's surface. "No! No!" I blurble and bang against the black surface. My eye presses against the keyhole.

"Hold on! Hold on!"

Dad shakes me awake. "Andrea! Andrea! Wake up!" He's still pushing on me. "Kiddo, are you okay?"

"I'm awake. I'm awake." I'm tangled in my sheet and blanket so that my arms aren't free. I claw like a cat trying to get loose. "My leg. Ow! My leg." I try to grab my leg but don't have the hands for it.

"Hold up, Andrea. Wait!" Dad holds my arms so I'll stop thrashing. "Let me help you."

"My leg hurts." I writhe; I just want to move my hand.

"Okay, okay. Let's look at your leg." Dad begins to untangle the blanket and sheet. Somehow I've completely wrapped myself around. I'm in a blanket cocoon.

"Ow! Ow!"

"Wow, kiddo, you really knotted yourself up here." He lifts my leg, peels back the wrap. He picks up a pillow from the floor and presses it against my back. He uses it to help me to roll. Then he lifts my broken leg and rests it on the pillow. "How are you doing? Keep breathing, kiddo."

I take a deep breath. How does breathing make the pain feel both better and worse?

"Dad, did I screw up my leg?" I stare at the ceiling. Partially because I'm afraid I've wrecked my leg, and partially because it hurts to move.

Dad lifts the newly freed sheet, scoots my pajama leg up a little, and gently moves my leg slightly to the left and slightly to the right. I'm grateful for his soft hands. "It looks okay. In fact it's kind of cool with its black, blue, green, and yellow tones."

"Dad!"

Dad snags my desk chair, sets it next to the bed and takes a seat. "So you want to tell me what you were screaming about? You about scared me out of my slippers!"

"It was just a dream." The clock reads 7:00 A.M. I'll be late for school if I don't move—now. With my leg still aching, I doubt I'll be on the fast track.

"Do you want to talk about it?" Dad scratches the back of his neck. This tells me he's pretty sure I don't want to, and he's hopeful that I will.

"A girl was in trouble." As a matter of habit, I grab Pedro off of my bedside table. He presses his cheek into mine. *Go on*, Pedro seems to say, *tell him.*

Dad waits.

"She was drowning. I tried to save her." Pedro's ears flop one forward, one back, then they reverse. "I swam toward her, but she disappeared. Then I couldn't save myself. I was trapped." I push both ears over Pedro's eyes. In this position, he's blind and deaf. Poor Pedro.

"Sounds frightening," Dad says. "I'm glad it was just a dream."

"It was a nightmare."

"I suppose it was." He taps the bed a couple of times. "You used to sleep so peacefully. I loved to watch you." He scratches his neck. "And you could sleep anywhere, in the car, the kitchen, on the floor, in the—"

"—Dad! That was a long time ago." Truth is, I haven't slept well in months.

"You're right. Nevertheless, you were the best sleeper." Dad pushes on his thighs while standing up. I've never understood why people do that.

"Wait. Don't go yet." I hold Pedro close, hoping the move will keep Dad from leaving.

Dad lowers himself back into the chair. "What is it, kiddo? You look so serious."

"What about Mom?"

Dad goes right to his memory of hair, running his fingers through it. "I was going to talk to you about that later." There is a long pause. "Mom wants to come home."

"I heard. If she wants to come home, does she get to, just like that?" I face Pedro at Dad so we both stare at him.

"Well, not 'just like that.' It's complicated." Dad runs his hand back and forth, back and forth over his bald head. His nose is scrunched. "She hasn't been convicted of a crime. We can't make her stay in the hospital, if she doesn't want to be there."

"What does she have to do to get treated?" Pedro turns back to me and snuggles up to my cheek. "Kill me?"

"Andrea!" Dad hits the bed hard, jostling me. "Please! Don't say that." He pinches the bridge of his nose. "I'm sorry. But please, don't talk like that." Dad sounds exhausted.

The sun is up now. Up and out. It hasn't been this sunny in days. Since the storm last week, the weather has opted for gray or wet, or both wet and gray. Surprisingly, I miss the gloom.

"Your mother is doing better. Apparently, the medications are helping."

Pedro hops down to Dad's elbow, which is resting on the bed. "Pedro wants you to know I didn't mean that about the killing thing."

Dad pets Pedro's head and looks at me. "I know this is really hard. It's hard for everybody, but especially you."

"Do you think Mom's ready? To come home?"

Dad grabs one of his hands in the other, and balances his wrists on his head. His arms stick out from his ears like a wire hanger. He leans back in the chair. "I just don't know. I hope so. I want to think so; I'm just not sure. In truth, none of us has any experience with this. Your mother included."

I watch a couple of birds hopping in the tree outside my window. "I miss her. I want her to come home, but I want her to be her old self—the way she was."

Dad closes his eyes, takes a deep breath. "Me too, kiddo. Me too."

"She didn't look good the other day. She looked dead." I hug Pedro back to my chest; just remembering, I feel ill.

"I know, she didn't look good at all. They said something happened with her medication. They had to adjust the dosage. She's better now."

"Really?"

Dad leans forward in his chair, resting his elbows on his knees the way Samantha does. "Really. I'm not saying she's healthy and there's no longer any sign of her illness. But she is much, much better." He puts his hand on mine. "I promise."

I chew the inside of my mouth. Soak up the heat from his palm.

"This is difficult, isn't it?" Dad turns my hand over so my fingers curl around his. I hold tight, then let go.

"Maybe, if she's better, she should come home." The birds are now hopping and twittering. They act as if it's May instead of November. Maybe she should come home.

"Dad, can we put a bird feeder outside my window?"

Dad chuckles. It is so nice to see him smile. Mr. Cheery hasn't been around for awhile. "That's a great idea." He gently slaps the bed. "You're a genius!"

"Yeah. Call me Einstein."

Dad gets up again, just as he did twenty or so minutes ago. "We're running a little late. So hop to it." He hops on one foot. "Ha! Hop to it. Get it?"

"Uh, yeah, Dad, I got it. Now go. Shoo." I wave him out of the room. He's just about to leave when I call him back one more time. "Dad?"

He's out the door but his head pokes back inside the frame. "What?"

"Has Margie called?"

He shakes his head. "No. I don't think she has." More of him comes back into the doorway. "Is everything okay with you two?"

"She's mad at me." Pedro is giving me a long look with his black, black eyes.

"Margie mad?" Dad, too, shakes his head like he has water in his ears.

"Yeah—" Birds have been flying in and out of the tree. There were two, then one, then three, now one again. "I was a jerk."

"First thing, when you get to school, find her. Friends like Margie, they're rare." Dad pats the doorjamb, and pulls his head back and disappears. I can hear him call, "Now get up! We're late! We're late, for a very important—" his voice trails off.

"All right." I give Pedro one more nose snuggle and place him on the bedside table. "Thank goodness you and Sean aren't mad at me." Then I begin the precarious task of nudging my way out of bed. Before the broken leg I was a get-up-and-go person. Now I'm a scoot-and-hobble girl.

While putting the Courage medallion in my memory box, I take Margie's butterfly necklace out. It is so Margie—light, carefree, beautiful. I'm going to ask her if I can wear it as a sign of our friendship. That is, if we're still friends. All of a sudden I can't get to school fast enough.

CHAPTER 21

Galumphing as fast as I can into school, I see Sean standing, waiting for me. He's wearing a blue-and-green-striped oxford, a navy blue tee and jeans. His hair hangs in front of his eyes. He looks really good.

"Hi, Sean." I'm sweating—can't tell if it's from nerves or exertion. "You didn't have to wait for me."

"No problem, I wanted to wait. Besides, being your sidekick gives me an official excuse to be late to class." Sean walks beside me toward my locker. "It's cool."

"I can't believe how late I am. It was hard getting up this morning." I hand some books to Sean and quickly close up my locker. "Did you see Margie today? Earlier?"

"I saw her, but she kind of avoided me. She's moody."

"No, she's not. She's mad at me is all." We are almost at the room for my first class. I stop short of the doorway, so no one will see us talking in the hall.

"Oh. That's too bad—" Sean nods and tucks his hair behind his ear. "Matthew keeps bugging me. He wants the four of us to go out on a date. Well, not the four of us—you and me, and Margie and he—you know what I mean." He turns away; I think he's blushing.

"Really?" I crane my neck to see into the classroom. I really should get in there. "Margie's not that mad. She'll want to go."

"Cool. You'll ask her then?"

"Definitely. I'll see her in Psych, and ask her then." I tilt my head toward the door. "I really should get to class."

"Yeah, me too. Although, this is more fun." Sean smiles.

I almost fall; my good leg buckles. How can I go out with a guy whose grin makes me tipsy?

Sean steadies me by placing his hand on my arm. "I haven't heard about your visit with your mom yet."

I glance left and right, everywhere that Sean isn't. "I really need to find Margie." The buzz of the lights jangles my nerves. "My mom was terrible."

"Oh." He uses the fingers of his free hand to comb his hair back. "Sorry. That must have been hard."

"Yeah—" I look up the hallway and down. "Plus she might be coming home soon."

"Wow. Even though she's sick?"

"Yeah. Well, no. Not if she's sick." The buzzing continues. I keep scanning the hall. "They say the medications will make her okay." I arrange my crutches so I'm ready to make that first step, like a sprinter on her mark. "I really need to get to class." It's silly but I want to get to English so that Psych will come quicker. That's nuts.

"Sure, sure. I'll see you in about 40 minutes—to take

you to your next class." He smiles that smile again. My leg wobbles like it's made of Jell-O.

"Okay." I wait for him to open the door, bring my books inside, but he just stands there, smiling. "Great—" I twist my hips toward the door and motion like I'm going to take a step with my crutches. "Sean? Earth to Sean?"

He snaps his head back and chuckles. "Sorry, I was lost looking at you." He quickly shakes his head. "That sounds stupid. Forget I just said that." He's blushing again. "Come on. Let's go."

Margie is going to be so excited about the double date. I can't wait to tell her. She has to forgive me for being a jerk. She just has to.

Psych isn't far from English, so I'll have a few minutes to talk with Margie before Mr. Portland shows up. I'm glad he has a free period before our class so he's not already in the classroom, waiting.

Sean waves a short wave at me, then heads for the door. He doesn't say anything, but looks at me, then at Margie, and back at me. His eyes are screaming, "Ask her. Ask her."

"Hi, Margie." My voice cracks.

No response.

I tear a piece of paper from my notebook, scribble on

it, and shield the words I write. She's not looking, but I do it anyway. I tap her on the shoulder. She takes a deep breath in, lets a long breath out.

"Please, Margie." I hold the folded piece of paper over her shoulder. This is a stretch for me. My leg doesn't like it.

Margie takes the note from me. She unfolds it with another loud breath, in and out. I can't tell, but I think she's reading what I wrote.

I know that I was awful. I love you and hope that you'll give me another chance to be a good friend—to be your friend.

I drew a couple of hearts on the bottom and added,

P.S. I have great, incredibly wonderful, fantastic news. You're going to like it.

"Great news?" At least the back of Margie's head is talking to me.

"Great, great news!"

Margie's shoulder twitches like she wants to turn around, but she catches herself. "I don't want you to be a jerk anymore."

"I promise." I write an X across my heart. "You couldn't see but I just crossed my heart."

Margie's shoulders rise and fall with another breath. "You hurt my feelings, McKane."

I tug at her shirt. "I know. And I'm *so* sorry." I tug again. "Please, Margie."

She doesn't pull away from me. She picks up the note, runs her finger across the page. She sits, breathes, waits. "You have good news?"

"I do." I nod, even though she can't see me.

"What is it?" Margie's head turns a little to the left. I bet she can see me out of the corner of her eye.

I lean forward over my desk. "Matthew wants to go out with you."

Margie turns around so fast that I rear back, surprised. "I should have told you that sooner, I guess."

"Yes. You should have." Margie has Pedro eyes again. "But tell me now."

"Matthew wants to ask you out, he's just too shy." My heart is beating so fast; it rushes relief to every muscle. I haven't lost my friend. "He wants the four of us, you and him, Sean and me, to go on a double date."

"Really? He wants to go on a double date?"

I nod. "Really." I want to laugh or dance—well, I can't really dance with my boot—but get up and hop around. "I wasn't kidding when I told you he liked you. He does; he really does."

Margie does a quiet little toe tap. "When? Where? What will I wear?"

"That brown sable shirt for sure."

"Yeah, or the green—" Margie stops herself.

"What?"

"You saw your mom?" Margie lays a hand flat on my desk. Smoothes it out.

"Yeah." I'm stunned by Margie's ability to switch from being happy for herself to thinking about me. One minute she's doing a happy dance because she's going on a date, and the next she's concerned about a friend. About me.

"How was it?"

"Bad." My throat gets tight. There's something about talking to Margie that brings up all the sadness that I've buried.

Margie puts her hand on my arm. "It'll be okay."

I shake my head. I'm not sure.

"She might come home soon," I sputter through my croaky throat.

"Oh, I see." Margie looks over her shoulder a couple of times. Mr. Portland should arrive shortly.

"Margie?" I am so close to tears I can taste them. "Can I ask you something? A favor?"

"Ask me—ask me anything."

I dig into my pocket and pull out her butterfly necklace. I wrapped it in tissue on the way to school. "Can I wear this—until my mom comes home?" I hold the necklace up for Margie to see.

Her face brightens when she sees the shiny silver pendant. She raises her hand so it rests in her palm. She closes her fingers around it for a second.

"Sure. Let me put it on you," she says, getting up from her desk.

She lifts the chain from my fingers and fiddles with the little knobby circle. I bend my head down so she can reach around my neck. I'm being knighted.

"It looks good on you." Margie stands back to admire the necklace. She's careful not to trip over my leg.

"Thanks." Now I think I'm blushing. My face feels red. "It'll remind me that no matter how weird things get with Mom, you're my friend."

Margie sits down and turns in her seat so she's facing me. She takes both my hands in hers. "Even when I'm mad at you, you're still my best friend. You always will be."

That causes a tear to roll down my cheek. I don't want to wipe it away because then everyone will know that I'm crying. There's something so obvious about the movement that erases a tear.

Right on cue Mr. Portland comes into the classroom, all normal and businesslike, drops his briefcase on his desk, and says, "Ready? Let's begin."

Before Margie turns around I touch the butterfly at my throat. "You're the best," I whisper.

Margie faces front. Mr. Portland writes a long list of mental disorders on the board. There are so many, he almost runs out of space.

I run the butterfly up and down the chain, *shh, shh, shh.* All those illnesses of the mind—bipolar disorder,

depression, autism, anorexia nervosa, bulimia, schizophrenia, on and on—they'd terrify me if I didn't have a
friend—a best friend.

Chapter 22

"I can't believe he likes me." Margie is putting on her makeup, moving in toward the mirror. It looks like a prism has fractured her at the point of her nose. I'm sitting on the toilet seat cover, leaning against the back wall, looking relaxed except for my booted foot. I represent a different kind of fractured.

"What do you mean?" Absent-mindedly, I spin the toilet paper roll.

"No one ever likes me. You they like, but not me." She stretches her mouth open so she can apply mascara more easily. I copy her, stretching my mouth open and closed.

"Margie, when are you going to get it? This 'boys like me and not you' thing is all in your head." I get up and hop to the sink, standing next to Margie so we're both looking in the mirror. "Except for Eddie Weasel, you and I have had the same number of boyfriends: zero."

Margie stops applying her makeup and looks at me in the mirror. "Maybe you're right. Though you'll always have Eddie." She turns back to her own reflection, all grins. "I can't believe Matthew likes me. That's all."

"Well, I can." Margie has long wavy red hair; it isn't a flat brown sheet like mine. She's beautiful. *And* she's the nicest person I've ever met.

"Aren't you wearing any makeup?" Margie waves her mascara wand at me.

"Moi?" I mock shock. "Actually I *am* wearing makeup. Can't you tell?" I bug my eyes, purse my lips, suck in my cheeks.

Margie pushes my shoulder.

"Hey, watch it with that thing." I hold up my hands to ward off the mascara saber.

"Let's get serious now. Are you bummed that we're going ice skating?" Margie lifts herself onto the sink counter.

I open my mouth to speak, but nothing comes out. Am I bummed?

"Maybe an eentsy, teensy little bit." I lean into the mirror, the way Margie was a little while ago. My face looks huge, just like my mother's. It was either the illness or the medication; something made my mother's face puffy and her eyes dull. I can't look at myself any more; I turn to Margie, touching the butterfly just below my throat.

"It'll be fun watching you wobble and shake your butt while Matthew wraps his arms around you." I hold my arms out and jerk my butt back and forth, although I almost lose my balance while pretending that I am.

"Andrea!" Margie hops off the counter.

"I mean, because he's trying to hold you up." I smile and give her an exaggerated air kiss.

Margie copies my back and forth wobbles. "Yep, no one will know I'm really an Olympic skater." She pretends to trip and falls forward toward the sink.

"Skating is the perfect ruse. Matthew will be all over you, making sure you don't fall." I've got to hand it to Margie. When it comes to matters of love, she's pure genius.

Margie closes up her mascara, finishes applying Scent of Summer, whatever that is, blush and lip gloss. "We don't have to go skating—"

"No, it's okay." I sneak the lip gloss and apply a layer. "Sean said he'd sit with me." I smack my lips the way Margie does.

Margie is still stuffing things into her purse when there's a knock at the front door.

"I've got it," Dad calls from the front room. He's probably been peeking out the window, just waiting for Sean and Matthew to show up. He got very jumpy when I told him that Matthew had his driver's license.

"Hello, Mr. McKane." Sean politely addresses my father. I listen in.

"Hello, Sean. How are you tonight?"

"Good. Good. Uh, Mr. McKane, this is Matthew. Matthew, this is Mr. McKane." Sean coughs. As I come around the corner, I see Matthew and Dad shake hands.

"Hello, Matthew, nice to meet you." Dad puts his hand on Matthew's back. "I hope you don't mind my asking, but how long have you had your license?"

"Dad—" I swing a couple of steps toward Matthew. "Ignore him. He's just being 'Dad.'" I lift my hands to make the quote symbol with my fingers, but have to abandon the idea when I almost drop both crutches.

"Oh, no problem. Ha." Matthew wipes his hands on his pants.

Despite his nerves, Matthew is the image of responsibility. His hair is short; his clothes are clean and pressed, but not too creased. As a senior, he's a few years older than we are.

"I've had my license for seven months and two weeks. Got it on my birthday." Poor Matthew, beads of sweat form on his forehead.

"He's a good driver, Dad." I hop closer to the door.

"I haven't had any accidents. No tickets. I even observe the speed limit." Matthew is on a roll now. I swear smoke is coming out of his ears.

"Enough, Dad."

Maybe Dad feels bad for Matthew, too. "That's great, son," he says and pats Matthew's shoulder. "Just great." Dad beams. "Now Sean—"

I groan.

"I've been meaning to thank you for helping Andrea out at school."

"It's no problem." Sean stands with his thumbs hooked in his pants pockets. He must hate this. "I'm happy to do it."

"Andrea may be able to lose her crutches soon. Isn't that great?"

"Yes, sir. That is."

Margie is prodding me in the back. She wants me to get us out of here.

I make my move, crutches precede me into the crowd, and everyone steps back. It's been that way since I broke my leg—everyone recedes as I approach.

"Enough with the Dad duties. We have to go." Sean opens the door for me. "The rink will be closed before we get there." I remember when I could approach the door, open it, and leave the house without thinking twice. Crutches have changed all that.

"Bye." I manage a small wave before clanking my way out the door. Everyone follows behind me. I hear a chorus of "Bye, Mr. McKane." It feels good to get outside. The air is cool, the stars incredibly bright. I breathe out in short bursts, sending smoke signals to the birds in the trees.

Margie gets in the front seat next to Matthew, and Sean and I, after futzing with my crutches, get in the back. The ends of the crutch stick over the back seat so that I feel like I'm looking over a fence at Sean. "I will be so happy to be rid of these."

He laughs.

"I don't know, I think I'll miss walking you to all your classes." Sean's eyes sparkle. He holds my hand.

"That's been the best part of this broken leg fiasco, for sure." I hold his.

Margie and Matthew are talking quietly. I can only see the side of her face, but she looks happy, really happy. Matthew is back to his shy self, but I can tell he's having a good time.

"Holy shit!" Matthew pumps the brakes and swerves; we all lurch forward. "What was that?"

"What? What happened?" Margie, Sean, and I speak as one.

"That crazy guy by the side of the road! He stepped into the street, right in front of me." Matthew looks back over his shoulder a couple of times. Strikes the steering wheel. "I could've killed him."

I sit up so I can talk to Matthew. "Stop the car. Catch your breath." Perhaps I inherited "911 genes" from my father.

"Are you crazy?" Matthew speeds up instead of stopping. "I'm not stopping near that nutcase!"

"Matthew—" Margie sits up in her seat. "Maybe you should pull over."

"No way." Matthew accelerates. "The guy almost jumped on the car."

"Matt!" Sean says. We are all sitting upright like car pegs in the game of *Life*.

"He's way back there. He's not going to hurt you." My words come out in punches. I grip and push on the back of the driver's seat.

"Shut up, McKane." Matthew speaks rapidly; his voice cracks.

"Hey!" says Margie.

"Slow down!" says Sean.

I slam into the back seat, fold my arms and stare out the window. Matthew doesn't get to call me McKane; he's the one who should shut up. Breathe, I remind myself. Breathe.

"What? I couldn't believe it. The guy was standing there by the side of the road, and right when I approached, he walked into the street." Matthew rubs his forehead as though he's in pain. "That's insanity. I could've run him ov—"

"Matt! Enough! We got it," Sean says. He leans forward so his chin almost rests on the back of the front seat. "Forget it! Okay?" he says quietly. It's like they are going to try and have a "guy talk" right here in the car, right between Margie and me.

"Yeah, okay." Matthew switches between looking forward, looking at Margie, then at Sean and me.

"Do you think we should call the police? I mean the guy isn't right. Right? Maybe he needs help." Matthew has slowed the pace considerably.

I'm glad for that.

Matthew holds his hand out for Margie. "Sorry. That was just so weird." Margie takes his hand; the car quiets.

I tap my leg, tick off each irritation.

"What would make somebody do that?" Matthew punctures the silence. He shakes his head like he's trying to erase an Etch-a-Sketch image.

"There are a million things that could make a person do that." Why did I say anything? I shouldn't speak when I'm mad.

"Like what?" Matthew sticks his neck up so that he can see me in the rearview mirror. I am tucked away in the corner back here.

"Well, mania, depression, bipolar disorder, psychosis, mental retardation, schizophrenia, to name a few." These were some of the illnesses Mr. P wrote on the board.

"Okay, we get the idea." Sean knocks my crutches while reaching for me. They are definitely in the way. I want to lose all these words I just said. Forget them and go back in time fifteen minutes, a week, a month, a year. I want to go back.

Matthew checks Sean and me out in the mirror, and repeatedly looks at Margie. He looks like a guy who knows that something has happened, but hasn't been able to figure out exactly what.

"Should we call the police? If the person's sick?" Even though he's tracking several different things, Matthew is doing a good job of driving.

We pull into the rink parking lot. I can hardly wait to get out of the car. As soon as we stop, seatbelts unbuckle and doors open. Everyone seems eager to step into fresh air.

"What do you think?" Sean slides my crutches out of the back and brings them around to my side of the car. My ankle is throbbing. After fighting my way out, I lean against the car and take in the wide, wide, wide-open sky. That's one good thing about parking lots—they open up the heavens so it's just you and the stars.

"How should I know? Because my mom's crazy, I'm supposed to know what to do when a guy jumps in front of a car?" I'm shaking, I don't know why. I'm not mad at Sean, but I'm acting like I am. I speak in barks.

"You're right." Sean reaches for me, but I lurch off the car and take a few strides to put myself in the middle of the driveway. I move away from Sean, whose hand is still extended, and away from Matthew and Margie, who stand shoulder to shoulder behind him.

I can hear Matthew say, "What happened? What's she pissed about?"

"I'll talk to her." Margie breaks away from the group and walks over to me.

"You okay?" Margie doesn't act angry, but she doesn't seem pleased either. "What's going on?" Her questions are sharp.

"I think there's something wrong with me." There,

I've said it. "Oh, shit, we can't talk about this now." Tears fill my eyes, my stomach squeezes.

"What's wrong?" Margie approaches me, but my wall of crutches keeps her from getting too close.

"I can't." I bend over. I'm incredibly hot and think I might throw up. Breathe, one, two, three.

"Don't freak out, Andrea. C'mon." She squats down in front of me so I can see her in my doubled-over state. "Not tonight. Please."

I nod. "Okay. I'm better." I stand. Margie does too. "Tell Matthew I had girl problems."

Margie lets out a "ha." "There *is* something wrong with you, if that's what you want as your cover."

"How do I look?" Margie's my mirror. I can tell by her reaction if I'm a mess.

"A little sensitive—pinch your cheeks."

"See, I do have girl problems. I hate this." I squeeze skin between my knuckle and thumb.

"Perfect." We turn to head back to the boys. Margie stops me for a moment. "Is there something wrong with you, really?"

Tears brim, I shake my head, I shrug my shoulders. I do not and cannot speak.

"We'll talk later." Margie presses her hand to her butterfly necklace that I am wearing. "You ready to see your sweetheart?"

Sean and Matthew talk, look over at us, talk some

more. I take a couple of deep breaths. Maybe it's a good thing I can't run. Otherwise I might run and run and run. And keep on running. "Yep, I'm ready."

We walk back to Sean and Matthew. "Sorry," I say. "I think it's something I ate."

Everyone laughs. I breathe relief.

"No problem." Sean walks over to me, and Margie to Matthew. They exchange places. "Everything okay?" Sean asks.

"Yeah." I'm not sure what else to say.

"I hope I didn't say anything—," Matthew takes Margie's hand, but speaks to me.

"No. Really. No problem." I hang on my crutches. Swing my bent leg back and forth. "We should call my dad, about the guy. He'll know what to do."

"That's a great idea." Margie takes Matthew by the hand and runs ahead, pulling him along. "Her dad's a 911 operator." They look like a large bird with outstretched wings.

"Sorry," I whisper, to Sean. "I hope I didn't mess things up."

"You broke your ankle. Your mom's sick." Sean hops on one leg for a step or two. He boxes the air. "Makes sense to me that you'd be mad sometimes." I wish I could put my arm in his, but with crutches, even walking side by side is difficult.

To change the subject I say, "I saw you run again on

Tuesday. You're more graceful every time I watch you." Sean doesn't say anything but smiles big. "How far did you run? I watched you for a couple of laps—you didn't show any signs of slowing or stopping. It was as though you could go forever."

"I'm training to run in the marathon. I think I ran nine miles—I've got a ways to go." Sean lifts his legs in an exaggerated running-in-place motion. "But those nine sure felt good."

"I bet." I'd be happy with nine *shh, shh, shh*, strides. I take one long crutch step, then another. Sean acts like he's jogging to keep pace.

Galumph, galumph, galumph. I am not graceful. But I am, sort of, running. Swing the crutches forward, then me, then the crutches. I go faster in order to catch up with Margie and Matthew—they've already gone inside. Sean keeps pace.

The stars are bright, the sky is clear, and Sean and I laugh and run. Well, sort-of run. The threat of foul weather has passed.

It's a beautiful night.

Chapter 23

"So, Andrea, how are you doing?" Samantha's voice sounds like the horizon, perfectly even.

"Okay, I guess."

"You guess?"

I sit up straighter; for some reason I was melting into the couch.

"I'm not falling down so much." I press the thumb of my left hand into my right. My good foot taps.

"That's good." Her voice is liquid, without waves.

"Yeah, I'm good. Everything has been going really well." I separate my hands, tucking them underneath my thighs. Trying to control them is futile; they need to be active.

"I'm glad to hear it." Samantha leans forward in her chair. "You seem nervous today. Can you talk about that?"

"Nervous?" I squeak.

Samantha nods, her mouth a straight line like her voice.

"If I'm nervous, it's just because things are going so well." I laugh. "I'm not used to that."

"I see."

"In fact, I think I'm ready to stop therapy." It's no use; I interlace my fingers and use a thumb to dig a hole in the palm of my hand.

"I see."

"What do you mean you see?"

"I understand that you want to leave therapy."

"I can, right? I mean, my mom can come home because she wants to, so I can stop therapy because I want to too, right?"

"Well, there are differences." Samantha nods. "Your mother is an adult, whereas you are still a dependent. The State has a responsibility to make sure that you're properly cared for."

"That's crap." My face gets hot. "The State isn't helping me at all."

"I agree, the State is often an ineffective caretaker." There isn't even a bump in Samantha's expression.

"What's wrong with you? You're like a robot." I pick up the egg that sits on the table, day in and day out.

"Andrea, put the egg down." Samantha doesn't move.

I toss the egg up and down in my hand. "I wonder if I dropped this, would it break like a breakfast egg?"

"Put it down." Even, not a ripple in tone.

"This is really pretty." I hold it up and turn it left, then right. "I like the houses, trees, and teeny people painted all bright colors, and going all the way around. It's cute.

Everyone in the village is happy." The people are so small they don't even have faces.

"Andrea—"

"I wonder if there is an asylum in this sweet town. Maybe this is the nuthouse." I hold up the egg so Samantha can see where I'm pointing. I tap, tap, tap the tiny blue house.

"That's enough." Samantha hasn't moved.

"Oh, now you sound like my mother. 'Stop what you're doing or else—'" My throat hurts from my imitation whine. The egg has heft. It's smooth, balanced, as it rolls in my palm—back and forth, up and down.

Samantha hasn't taken her eyes off me. She taps her thumb on the arm of her chair.

I continue to roll the egg—I want to see how far out on my fingertips I can get it to go without having it fall off.

Samantha sits, watches, and drums.

I roll the egg out, watch it return, roll it out.

Samantha sits, watches, and drums.

"Are you having fun?" I ask. I'm getting very good at the egg thing. I can almost roll it onto the tips of my fingers, so that it's balanced there.

Samantha watches.

"Come on, you have to admit this is cool." I continue to practice. "Look at what I can do."

Samantha gets up, goes into her closet, and comes out

with a pad of lined paper and a pen. She sits back down, looks at me, and starts to write.

I stop rolling the egg.

"What are you writing?" I demand.

Samantha continues to write. Taking moments to raise her eyes toward me, then returning them to the paper.

I put the egg back in the stand.

"Look. I'm not rolling the egg anymore." I lean forward, as though I can see and read what Samantha has written. Even with Superman eyes, I don't think I'd be able to decipher her faraway and illegible scrawl.

Samantha writes, looks up, looks down, continues to write.

"Please tell me what you're writing. I'm asking nicely. Please?" I have to know what she is writing. Why won't she tell me?

"What are you afraid of?" I hear a voice. It sounds like me. Did Samantha just speak? She's watching me; it looks like she's talking, but I can't hear anything. "What are you afraid of?" the voice asks again.

"Are you talking to me?" I ask Samantha.

I see her lips move, but I can't hear anything.

"What are you afraid of?" The sound is out of sync with Samantha's mouth. It's like a very bad video recording.

"Shut up!" I yell to the ceiling. The voice isn't coming from above, I'm not sure where it's coming from.

Samantha moves in closer, she even pulls her chair forward. I can read her lips. "Breathe, Andrea. Breathe in—one, two, three. Breathe out—one, two, three." She puts one hand on her abdomen and gestures to me with the other, to breathe along with her. I follow her lead.

"Andrea? Can you hear me?" Samantha sounds like she's under a thousand blankets, but I can hear her. I press my head with the heel of my hand. Something is very wrong.

"Andrea? Look at me." I look at Samantha. She nods; she seems relieved that I am able to understand what she is saying.

I feel trapped in a thick cloud. I can hear and see Samantha, but she's foggy and smothered. I'm underwater. The words *hold on! hold on!* scream inside my head.

"There's something wrong with me," I whisper.

"What's wrong with you?" Samantha's words float between us.

"Don't you know?" I grab a throw pillow and muffle a scream with it. I don't feel any better. I've got to get out of here. "Tell me!" I struggle to stand on my one foot, pick up my crutches, "No, don't tell me, I don't want to know. Just forget it. Forget everything."

"Andrea, sit down."

"I can't. There's something wrong with me. Terribly wrong." As much as I want to go, I can't move.

"Andrea, you're in a dissociative state. I need for you

to sit down." Samantha helps me to put my crutches back down.

"I can't," I say, as I sit. "I can't." I wrap my arms around myself. Samantha hands me a glass of water and a blanket she gets from her closet. I drink and wrap myself up. I'm acting like it's freezing cold and I'm holding a cup of cocoa. I imagine a fire blazing in front of me.

"I need you to use words." Samantha sits on the edge of her chair, her elbows on her knees. "Talk to me."

Samantha is moving in and out of focus. I'm sighting her through a viewfinder.

"Andrea?"

"What am I afraid of? That's what the voice kept asking me." I shiver.

"What are you afraid of?"

"I'm, what I'm, I mean—"

"It's okay, Andrea, take your time." Samantha taps her fingers a couple of times. "Let's start again, more simply. Who am I?"

"You're Samantha." It's a dumb question, but I actually feel good that I know the answer.

"Very good." Samantha smiles. I feel the snake in my belly uncoil and evaporate. I start to shake. Every bone rattles.

"What's happening? I can't stop shaking." I feel like I'm holding a jackhammer five times my size.

"It's okay. That's a good sign." Samantha picks up the glass of water she poured for me earlier. She takes my rattling hand and puts it around the cup.

"Wh-, wh-, why?" My teeth are chattering, too.

"Take a sip," Samantha instructs. "You are coming back together—pulling yourself together."

"I, I, I don't under-, under-, understand."

"A little more. That should calm the shaking." Samantha mimes lifting a glass to her lips.

I do as I'm told, as I'm shown. The shaking melts into mild shivering.

"Samantha, what's wrong with me?" Tears drip down my cheeks.

"You have PTSD—Post Traumatic Stress Disorder."

"PTS what?" I hug the pillow to my chest and rock back and forth. I want Pedro.

"PTSD. It is something that happens to people when they have experienced a trauma."

I'm sobbing now, or crying. I bend over the pillow and unleash the choked back tears.

"Do I have to go to the hospital?"

"Because you have PTSD?"

For a moment I break through, breathe air. Then there is a tug from below and I resubmerge.

"Yes," I say into the heart of the pillow. I hope Samantha can hear me.

"No, you don't need to go to the hospital. Is that what you are afraid of?" Samantha moves her chair closer again. She is near and bending forward. "Many people, maybe even most people who experience severe trauma, develop PTSD. Do you understand what I'm saying?"

I nod.

"However, they aren't hospitalized." Samantha moves her right foot a half-inch to the left. "That you just noticed that I moved my foot and felt anxious because I changed position, that's called hypervigilance."

I don't nod; for a moment, I don't breathe.

"Hypervigilance is when someone watches others, noticing everything about them. Like how you notice when I shift in my seat, when I move forward, when I move back; that's all hypervigilance."

My cheeks heat up. I'm embarrassed that Samantha knows that I see things about her. "And that's PTSD?"

"That's one symptom. Insomnia, nightmares, dissociation, flashbacks, outbursts of anger—those are some of the others."

"Oh. Is PTSD the reason why I keep having the dream about drowning?"

"I think so, yes." Samantha presses her fingertips together, rests her elbows on her knees, then leans forward. Things are returning to normal.

"You said, earlier, that I was in a dissociative state. So that was PTSD?"

"Again, I think so. That's a physiological and mental state. The body thinks it's re-experiencing the trauma while the mind gets foggy and disconnected."

I nod my head up and down. Fast. I'm almost bouncing in my seat. "Everything was thick, I couldn't get through. It was a lot like my drowning dream."

I rub my leg. It aches, or maybe I'm just anxious. It feels good, though, that Samantha understands, that my experiences, and my feelings, have a name, and that I don't need to go to the hospital. Again, I surface.

The rug is soft and clean right now—a good sign. "Samantha?"

"Yes."

"Does this mean—I mean am I—I don't know how to say it." I'm erasing the corner of the pillow, rubbing at it.

"Try. Take your time, —breathe, —relax." Samantha puts her hand on her abdomen again and so do I.

"When I start to ask the question, I just want to cry."

"I understand. It scares you. Just try." Samantha sits back, as if the space will help me. It does. I focus on my favorite square in the rug. My "hypervigilance" monitors every breath that Samantha takes, and notices the window in the neighbor's house, and the fact that there is a bird hopping along the eaves of the roof.

"Am I—" I take a couple of deep breaths. "Am I crazy? Am I like my mom?" This curls me over the pillow, and the tears run down the inside edge of my nose once again.

"No, Andrea. PTSD is not schizophrenia."

"But I heard a voice."

"Dissociation can have the effect of making thoughts seem like they are being spoken out loud. Psychotic voices, the kind that your mother hears, are typically unrelenting. They keep up a steady commentary of intrusive thoughts. To me, you didn't appear to be hearing voices nonstop. Were you?"

"No." I dry my tears. "Not unrelenting." I sit up a little straighter. "It was just one question." I look at Samantha. "'What are you afraid of?' That was the question."

Samantha nods. "It's a good question to ask yourself."

"I'm afraid of—" I take a couple of those big swallows that hurt going down. "—being like Mom. Being sick." My gulps pop in my ears.

"It's scary and difficult having a mom who's ill." Samantha touches my knee. "But you are not schizophrenic."

She gets up and goes into her closet. I hear drawers opening and closing.

"Today you have earned this medallion." She hands me a metal circle, on it is engraved the word *Strong*. "Your mind and heart, Andrea McKane, are incredibly strong. I know this is tough work, but you are up to the task."

It's like I've just had a medal pinned to my shirt.

I rub at my eyes with my shirt-sleeve, like a five-year-old who hasn't learned to use tissues. As I settle on the couch and Samantha sits back in her chair, her voice, once again, has the calm and clarity of the horizon in the early morning. Light pushes away the darkness and the fog begins to clear.

I feel strong.

CHAPTER 24

"Remember, the doc said take it easy." Dad ties orange and yellow balloons to my crutches, now retired and abandoned to the corner. "No overdoing it." He skips when he walks. I limp around the kitchen.

Dad hasn't been this bubbly in weeks.

"I'm just walking from the sink to the fridge; I'm hardly overdoing it." Admittedly, I am walking back and forth, back and forth. I keep thinking of things to pull from the fridge—ketchup, pickles, onions—just for the chance to take a step or two without crutches. After all, I am walking on my own two feet. Well, one foot and one walking boot. Oops, I forgot—relish, mustard, rolls—back and forth I go.

"Well, sit if your ankle starts to hurt—at all." Dad moves quickly from here to there. He slide steps like a skater and holds his hands up as though he's dancing an old person's dance, something from a Fred Astaire movie. He's humming, too.

"I think *you* should take it easy. You're way too excited." I slice the onions, squinting my eyes, hoping that I can keep from crying. I've cried or wanted to, at least once a day, every day, for weeks. I'm due for a dry spell. Nevertheless, here I am, tears dripping from my chin. Darn onions.

"Too excited? There's no such thing. My kid is walking on her own two feet, crutch free. If that doesn't call for dancing, nothing does."

"Right, Dad, maybe nothing does." We both are light on our feet, light in our banter. I'm sure my dad knows I'm teasing.

"When will the gang be here? I promise I'll stop dancing when they arrive."

"Thank God." I place the onion slices around the edge of the plate, then begin slicing the tomatoes. "They'll be here anytime." Margie, Matthew, and Sean are coming over to help me celebrate walking. Walking on two feet.

On cue there's a knock at the door.

"I'll get it," Dad says.

"No. Wait. Let me." I wipe my hands on the kitchen towel. There were so many things I couldn't do while I was using crutches—like answering the door—that I don't want to miss a single opportunity. In time I'm sure this will change.

"Of course. Of course."

I walk on tender feet, but I walk.

"Welcome to McKane Manor," I say, opening the door and offering a deep bow in my best butler imitation.

"You're walking!" Margie bubbles like Dad, although she literally hops. "You're walking!" She gives me a hug and almost knocks me over. I'm still fragile and unsteady on my feet. "Oops." She gives me another hug, one of those patty-pat ones.

"Get in here." I pull on her jacket sleeve.

Sean enters next. He has his thumbs hooked into his front pockets. I know him well enough to understand he does this when he's not sure what to do with his hands. "Hi," he says, his shoulders raised high.

"Hi."

Then Matthew enters. I can see his shy self drop away and the "I-know-how-to-act-with-adults" self take its place. It's an almost seamless transition. I'm very impressed.

"How does it feel?" he asks, pointing at my foot, now planted firmly on the ground. We've had a few awkward moments with each other since the rink, but mostly that night was a long time ago.

I take a deep, easy breath in. "It feels great!" I answer, releasing all the pent-up air—months of it—as I do.

Sean reaches out to close the door that I've been holding open. I take his hand in mine; so simple, so easy. "Like this." I squeeze Sean's hand. "Being able to use my hands for more than moving my crutches."

"Yeah," Sean responds. "This is better."

Dad calls from the kitchen. "Everyone into the living room. The *Chariots of Fire* dinner smorgasbord is almost ready." Dad came up with the idea of having my friends over, serving hamburgers, and watching an old movie about Olympic runners as a way to celebrate my liberation from crutches. He said we had to see this movie.

Matthew starts to move forward, then hesitates. "Does your dad know about the guy who jumped out when I was driving?" I guess, below the cool, he's still a little nervous.

"Yeah. We read about the guy in the paper, and I told Dad we saw him." I'm trying to reassure Matthew. I don't want something made of nothing. "Really, he's fine about the whole thing."

"What did the paper say?" Margie asks, taking Matthew's hand.

"The guy has Alzheimer's, and he ran away from home. He was disoriented." I'm getting tired standing here. Not used to spending so much time on my feet.

"I just didn't see him," Matthew says.

I'm beginning to understand why he got so upset that night. He felt responsible for our safety—and the man's too.

"It's okay. You did great. Look we're all still here." I tug my gaggle of friends toward the living room. "Now, come on. Let's go." I pull Sean, he follows, and Margie leads the way for Matthew.

Sean and I sit on the couch where I have a footrest set up. Matthew and Margie sit on the love seat. "You have a nice home," Matthew says.

"Thanks. I should take you on a tour. Really though, except for the bedrooms, you've practically seen the whole house. It's small, but cozy." I lean against Sean's shoulder. I think I'm making him nervous. He doesn't know that my dad is relaxed about most things, as long as I'm responsible.

"I like your house, too," Sean says, "it doesn't feel small at all." Sean acts like a guitar string whose peg has been turned. I haven't seen him like this before, but then I've never been to his house, nor has he spent any time in mine. I've heard that Sean's father doesn't give him much room to move. Maybe my house does feel spacious to him.

"It works." I begin the process of getting up. It is still a process since I'm not yet one hundred percent; I'm not back to normal yet. "I'm going to help my dad. I'll be right back."

"I'll go." Sean sits up.

"No." I speak much too abruptly. "Sorry. It's just that every chance I get, I walk." I step away from the couch, turn around, and step back. "I could do this all night."

"No, she can't." Dad calls from the other room. "'Light walking,' those were the doc's words."

Margie gets up and follows me into the kitchen. "This should be fun," she says, grabbing a bowl of chips. "You're brilliant for thinking of it, Mr. McKane."

"Yeah, Dad, thanks." My dad is really smart—in ways that surprise me.

Dad is sliding burgers onto buns onto plates. "It isn't every day that one gets to invite half of the Hayworth High Track Team over for dinner. It's a great honor."

"Ha. Obviously Andrea didn't tell you that anyone can make the track team. Now that she's walking without crutches," Margie tilts her head in my direction, "she'll be hobbling laps with the rest of us."

"Oh, no, she won't." Dad points his spatula at Margie, then at me.

"Don't worry, Dad, I'll limit myself to the quarter-mile sprint."

Margie leaves the kitchen with the bowl. "I've got the chips," she calls over her shoulder.

"Do you need help?" I ask Dad, picking up the condiment tray.

"Nope, I'm good. Go on," Dad urges me out of the kitchen. "Be with your guests. I'll bring the burgers right in."

I return to the living room. Margie is putting the DVD in the player. Matthew seems to be intently, maybe too intently, watching Margie bend over to put in the disk. Sean's reading the back of the DVD case.

"What does it say? Anything good?" I put the tray on the coffee table and take my seat next to him.

"It's a true story about two British runners. It won Best Picture in 1981."

"Yeah, my dad knows all the old movies."

Dad enters carrying a couple of plates piled high with cheeseburgers and pickles, and puts them on the table in front of Margie and Matthew. He hurries out and back, carrying plates for Sean and me.

"Okay. You kids have everything you need?" He picks up the DVD remote and presses "Play."

"Yep, Dad, we're good."

There is a chorus of satisfied "Mmm-mmms" and "These are delicious."

"Okay, I'll be in the kitchen if you need anything."

"Thanks, Dad," I say.

"Thank you, Mr. McKane," says everyone else.

We eat and watch. We eat and watch and lean into each other. I take Sean's soft hand in my own, and carefully examine the life, love, and career lines imprinted in his palm.

"Hey, Andrea, this movie is good. The food, too," Matthew says. "Thanks for inviting us."

"Yeah, McKane, we haven't watched a movie and just hung out in so long." Margie munches a couple of chips to make her point. "This is great."

I can walk, I'm happy, and I don't feel nauseous. This is a first.

"I've got it," Dad calls when the phone rings.

"I'm like Liddell," says Sean, "I run because I was born to run."

"It says here you were born to play basketball." I point at one of the short scraggly lines near his thumb.

"Yeah, but this one says I was born to run." He points to the thick, long, deep line near his ring finger.

"I see. That one is more serious, isn't it?"

"Exactly." Sean nods his head. "Now let me see what you were born to do." He takes my palm in his. "Look, you have a strong 'born to run' line too."

"So I do." I hold up my bum leg. "At least it didn't evaporate with this."

"No, that's just a false start. Now you need to reset, and wait for the starter pistol to refire."

"Hey you two—" Margie shushes us. "We're trying to watch a movie over here."

"Sorry." I raise my shoulders in apology.

Dad enters. "Andrea," he whispers.

I look over the back of the sofa to where he's standing, holding the phone. "Yeah?"

"It's your mother," he holds up the phone. "She needs to talk with you. I'm sorry for interrupting."

Sean, Margie, and Matthew all look at me. I look at the "born to run" line in my palm.

"You okay?" Sean asks.

"Yeah, fine. It's just a phone call." Sean helps me get up from the couch. My limp is worse, and my leg hurts more now than it did just five minutes ago.

I take the phone from Dad and head to my bedroom. Pedro joins me and listens in on the call.

"Hi, Mom."

"I'm sorry to disrupt your party."

"What's wrong?" Pedro's ears pop straight up. That didn't come out quite right.

"Well—" There is a scratchy sound as though she almost dropped the phone. "Nothing is wrong. This is the only time I'm allowed to call."

"Oh," I say.

Silence weaves between us. Behind her I can hear someone yelling. Maybe it's George.

"Well, I should get to the point. I'm sure you want to get back to your friends."

I wait.

"Andrea, I'm going to come home on Monday."

I take a deep breath in and let it out slowly, one, two, three.

"For a visit?" Breathe in, breathe out.

"No. For good, I hope."

"Are you okay?" Pedro nuzzles against the phone; he listens.

"Yes, sweetie, I'm fine. The medicine they have me on, the new medicine, has been working well. I feel good." She sounds more like my mom than she did the last time I talked with her.

I wait. I think.

"Is it set? Are you definitely coming home?" I ask. Pedro is hopping around on my gut. He jumps higher and higher and higher, until I squish him down.

"Yes. Yes it is. But, I want you to know, I'm doing fine. The doctor said I was ready."

"That's good."

"I'm anxious to come home—to be there for you."

"Yeah. I've missed you." Pedro is squiggling back and forth in my hand. He wants me to let him up, but I won't.

Mom coughs into the phone. It is a loud static burst. The screaming in the background intensifies. "I can hardly wait. I'll make you your favorite dinner."

"Do you know what it is?"

The yelling near my mother intensifies. "I'm sorry. I've got to go. I'll see you Monday." There is a banging sound. "I love you, Andrea. I'm okay now, you'll see." There's a click, then all the noise stops.

"It's fried chicken, green beans, and mashed potatoes," I say into the dead phone.

Pedro hops back to his spot on the bedside table. I limp back to my spot on the couch. I snuggle close to Sean.

"Are you okay?" He wraps his arm around me. "You're shivering."

"Could you get me some water and the blanket that's over there on that chair?"

"Sure. Sure." He jumps up, wraps the blanket around my shoulders, gets the water. He sits back down.

"You okay?" Margie pulls away from Matthew's arm.

"I'm fine." I pull my legs up onto the couch, even the broken one, and curl into Sean. "Let's just watch the movie."

Sean puts his arm around my shoulders and I sit, shivering, warming myself with imaginary cocoa in front of an imaginary roaring fire.

"You're okay though, right? Should I get your dad?"

"No. I'm fine." I pull myself together, tighter.

Samantha told me that, for some people, PTSD is like a series of storms passing through town. She said I might find myself ducking for cover and that's okay; it's a perfectly normal response.

I don't like bad weather, but, if the rain is going to hammer at the roof and the wind is going to push at the windows, this is the place where I want to be. I shake like a dog just out of water.

Sean turns to me, makes eye contact. "You're sure you're okay?"

"Yep. Just hold me." I sneak my hand out from underneath the blanket and place it on top of the one Sean has wrapped around my shoulder. He settles back in his seat and hugs me closer. He brings me in from the cold.

CHAPTER 25

It isn't easy to watch Margie, Matthew, and Sean run laps around the track when all I can do is sit on the bench, cheer, and clap as they round the bend. But it's better than going home.

Mom and Dad have returned from the hospital by now. Mom has probably already started to prepare her special meal, whatever it is. Dad and I planned on having a small celebration dinner to welcome her home. She liked the idea, except that she wanted to do all the cooking.

"Looking good, Margie!" I yell through a megaphone made with my hands. The weather is approaching cold. The great pines dig their saw teeth into the marbled blue and white. Margie runs a few feet past me then stops, doubles over. She's breathing hard, exhaling plumes of white.

"What ever possessed me to take up running?" she heaves, bent, hands on her knees.

"Hmm, I think he's coming around the far turn right now."

"Oh, yeah. Did I mention," she wheezes, "that I love to run." She plops down next to me, still struggling for air.

Matthew runs by us, his short, muscular legs carry him forward like a tiger. I can almost hear the *shh, shh, shh* as he passes. Margie bends forward and spits under the bench.

"Eww." I lift my feet like I'm avoiding high water.

"I hate it when guys spit," Margie says. "I wish it didn't feel so good." Her color returns, her breathing relaxes—the benefits of spitting.

"I wonder if it has healing properties."

"We know it feels good." Margie covers her spit spot by sliding dirt onto it with her toe.

"Looking good, Sean!" I yell through my hand-megaphone; steam funnels through my fingers. He glides across the track with long legs, long strides; he's a greyhound. When he passes I hear the *shh, shh, shh* as though I, myself, were running. He approaches, waves, and is gone. "Someday, pal. Someday you and I will run together," I mumble to Sean's beautiful back and his long legs. My shoulders droop a bit.

"No doubt about it." Margie puts her hand on my shoulder. "You'll be out there soon enough."

"I didn't realize how much walking would make me want to run." I spit on the ground between my feet, even though I have nothing to spit for. "I can hardly wait until I'm done with this boot."

"Hold your horses. You don't want to hurt yourself." Margie talks to the pile of dirt and rock she's built with her toes.

"Yes, Mother." I imitate Eeyore's drone.

Margie searches the track for Matthew, smiles when she finds him. "Running is also great for the bystander."

"Ha! Yep, it's a beautiful sport all the way around." I draw a track oval in the air. Margie and I wave at Jim and Mike, our track teammates. They don't know me, but they wave anyway.

As soon as they pass, Margie spits one more time. "Did I tell you, I hate it when guys spit?" She smiles, tamps down the scuff of dirt.

"Okay. Enough," I say.

"Yes, Boss." Margie pushes my shoulder. I collapse on the bench as though she's knocked me over.

"Now let me watch this gorgeous runner finish his run." Like a lookout, Margie scans the track in search of Matthew.

"Is Sean almost finished?"

"Very funny. I was thinking of the other gorgeous runner. The more mature one."

Now it's my turn to push Margie on the shoulder.

While sitting, I lift my legs one after the other, taking a couple of strides through the air in front of me. I stop short and put my arm on Margie's shoulder. "Thanks for asking Matthew if he'd give me a ride home. I didn't want to leave when school ended." She really helped me out; I'm in no hurry to get home. We talk while watching the graceful runners on the track.

"Oh, sure. He's happy to do it." Margie breaks her gaze away from Matthew to look at me. "What do you think it will be like? Home, I mean?"

"I don't know." I shake my head; keeping my eyes on the track. "Mom sounded pretty good. Almost like before." Margie turns back to the track. I holler, "C'mon, Sean!"

"You're gaining on him!" Margie yells to Matthew.

"Looking good, Matthew!" More clouds emerge from my megaphone.

"Great legs, I mean stride!" Margie adds although she isn't even watching the track.

I shrug my shoulders, getting back to the question. "If her medicine works, maybe home will be like—home."

Margie puts her arm around my shoulder and hugs me. "You deserve to have your mom back. Your real mom."

Sean runs down the stretch, throws out his chest, lays back his arms and head like the runners in *Chariots of Fire*. Margie and I applaud, hoot, and holler. Sean collapses on the track, flops to his back, again like the runners in the movie.

"You won! You won!" I reach out to offer him a hand up.

"I certainly did!" Instead of getting up, he gently pulls me down to the track. I lay on my back next to him, his arm my pillow. We watch the trees as they saw at the edges of the sky. The wide-open sky. "I don't think I've ever looked at life from this perspective before."

"No? Oh, it's great. There's so much space. From here, I think I can run to the Sun and back. Nothing is in my way."

I take a moment and note the clear shot from here to there. "Sean?"

"Yeah?"

I roll over so I am looking at him, watching his face. "You're beautiful."

He looks at me, brushes my hair behind my ear. "What?" His cheeks are brushed pink.

"You heard me," I answer.

He looks to the left, then right, then lifts his head so he can whisper near my ear, "Okay, but don't say it so anyone else hears you." He kisses me.

"Sealed with a kiss, eh." I turn back over, lying in the crook of Sean's arm.

"I had to make sure you wouldn't be saying those 'beautiful' things to anyone else."

"Hey you two, stop hogging the track." Matthew jogs toward us. He pretends to trip over us and takes wild windmill steps the last few feet, then pretends he falls as he lies down on the track. Margie joins him.

The four of us lie on the pink gravel and breathe in open space, nothing from here to there, and breathe out clouds of white.

"McKane, thanks for the lesson in tripping and falling. I like the view from down here," Matthew says.

"No problem. A change of outlook is always good."

"Life from the ground up, that's perfect," Matthew says.

It won't be long before someone moves, before someone says, "It's time to go." I know it will happen; it's inevitable, after all. I'll have to pick myself up, dust myself off, and head for home. But until then, the sky is gorgeous: it's brilliant, cool and blue. It's wider than the widest reach and protected by a circle of giant pines.

There's no better place to be.

Chapter 26

I like everything to be the same, all the time. Predictable. Routine. That's why, everyday, when I come home, I drop my backpack on the chair in the foyer, and go into the kitchen to hunt for something to eat. Today, of all days, I probably should have followed in my previous footsteps—exactly. Instead, I stick my pack on the chair and head for my bedroom.

"Hi, kiddo, we're in here." Dad calls from the kitchen. I flinch. Samantha said I might be jumpy. She was right.

"Hi, Dad." Oops. "Hi, Mom, Dad."

"Hi, sweetie." Mom is home.

Breathe in and out; be normal.

"What's for dinner?" I walk into the kitchen, look in the fridge.

"I've made pork chops, potatoes, and peas. Sorry about the peas, I know they aren't your favorite." Mom continuously wipes her hands in the towel, over and over and over again.

"It's okay, I like peas now. They've kind of grown on me." At least she got the potatoes right.

"Grown on you? Oh my God, where?" Dad pats his chest, peeks into the collar of his shirt. He's being his typical, goofball, self.

"Please cut the corn, Dad."

"First peas, now corn. What vegetable will I have to cut next?" Dad is holding his hands to his face and batting his eyelashes. I'm trying not to laugh, so I roll my eyes and pretend I'm too cool for these food group jokes.

"Do you need any help, Mom?" I don't mean to change my tone, but I do. The laugh drops out of my words, and I sound ever so serious.

"No, sweetie, I've got it all under control. We should be ready to eat in about 15 minutes, if you want to freshen up."

Freshen up? I'm not sure what she means. "Okay, I'll be back in a few minutes." I go to my room and flop on my bed. I want Pedro to give me a pep talk. "Pedro, everything's going to be okay, isn't it?" I whisper to him. He nods. "She looks good, more like herself." Pedro nods. "Dad seems happy." Pedro nods. "Mom's home, and everything is just like it was." Pedro stares at me with his onyx eyes. "I said, 'Everything is just like it was.'" Pedro stares, unblinking. "Well, everything else is true." Pedro nods and hops back to his spot on the bedside table.

I take my box off of the dresser. I touch each item—the Freedom, Courage, and Strong medallions, the wishing stone, my sneaker lace, and the photo of my mother and me. We were so happy then.

From the top drawer of my desk, I take the crumpled piece of paper that Margie gave me weeks ago, the one on which she wrote *We all know and we love you anyway.* That finds its way into the box as well.

I touch the butterfly pendant hanging around my neck. The silver is cool and bright, the butterfly in silent flight.

I don't know what my mom means by freshen up, but this is what it means to me: to remember that I am brave and strong, that I am free.

There's a knock at my door. For the first time in a long time, I don't know who it is.

"Come in." I close the lid on the box.

"Andrea?" Mom enters. She rubs the spot below her throat where the butterfly hangs on me. I copy her gesture and touch Margie's pendant. "You're so beautiful." Mom looks from me, to behind me, to the side. She surveys the room. "Do you mind if I sit?" She points at the bed.

I limp over to smooth out the bed cover, an unnecessary act, as I made my bed before I left for school. "Sure. I mean, no." I stand at the side not sure whether to sit or not. Not sure if I want to.

Mom sits, stares at the hardwood floor. "I know this has been difficult for you." She looks up at me, then back at the floor. "I'm so sorry about all the things I did to you."

My leg throbs. I lean as though I'm about to fall.

Mom pats the bed next to her. "Please, sit." She tucks her hair, black with hints of gray, behind her ear. "I want to start over." She takes my hand, lays my fingers on top of hers. "I think this medicine I'm taking is good. I feel more like myself." She turns away to cough. "Except for the dry mouth." She pushes at her lips with her tongue.

The room is melting. "I'm glad." I pinch my leg to keep from swirling away. "That you feel good." I pinch more and harder. "I am."

"Remember when we went skiing up at Snow Valley? Margie came along, and Dad and I had to lure the two of you back to the cabin with cocoa and a warm fire?" Mom puts her arm around my shoulder. "You didn't want to stop skiing."

No, we didn't. That was when I first fell in love with the *shh, shh, shh* sounds of being in motion. "That was fun."

"It was." Mom draws my hair back over my shoulder. "We should go again."

As I look at her, she smiles a broad smile. Then I glance at my leg.

The smile erases. "Later. I meant later." Mom pushes on her thigh, as I push on mine.

"It's okay." I put my hand over hers, for just a second.

"Dinner must be ready." Mom stands abruptly, steps toward the door, then turns to face me. "I love you, Andrea." She presses her hand to the imaginary butterfly at her throat. "I'm so sorry I hurt you." She retreats through the door.

"I love you, too," I say, not sure if she can hear me.

Sometimes I wish my mom was always one way or the other. The mom who just left my room is the one I miss. But I didn't get to be with her because I was so afraid the other one would show up. Nothing is predictable right now; nothing is the way I like it to be.

"C'mon, kiddo. Grub is getting cold." Dad's hum gets louder and softer as he walks back and forth between the kitchen and the dining room.

Nothing is the same, except for Mr. Consistent. Right now, Dad's song-and-dance mood, day in and day out, doesn't bug me so much.

CHAPTER 27

The phone rings. I almost jump out of my skin. "I'll get it." Gosh, I hope these jitters don't last much longer.

"Hello," I say into the phone.

"Hey, how's it going?" Margie whispers.

"It's Margie. I'll be in my room." I can't wait until I don't feel the need to announce to Dad and Mom everything I do. I'm bugging myself.

"Sure, kiddo. No problem." Dad took the night off from work, it being Mom's first night home and all. He and Mom watch TV.

I close my bedroom door and lay back on my bed. "You still there?"

"Yeah, yeah. So, how is it?"

"It's okay."

Margie doesn't say anything for a beat or two.

"Margie?" There are globs of spider web in a couple of corners of my room. It's been awhile since I've vacuumed, I guess. "Are you there?"

"What do you mean, 'It's okay?'" Margie is doing something else while we're on the phone. But I can't tell what.

"Mom. She's acting normal." I can see myself in the light reflected off the darkened window. Fall and winter are great, but the early nights give me the shivers.

"Cool. I wish my mother was normal." Drawers slam.

"What are you doing?" I pull the blanket at the foot of my bed up over my legs.

"I'm picking out shirts to cut up." Margie's breathing gets heavier and heavier.

"What?" I have no idea what Margie is talking about; even so, this is better than watching TV with Mom and Dad.

"I hate this!" Margie throws things; at least that's what it sounds like.

"Stop." I grab Pedro and hold him up to the phone, so he can hear. "Just stop."

Now the noises drop away. Margie's breath becomes even and quiet. Margie always runs to get help for me, and I apply the brakes in order to help her.

"Okay. I'm better," she says.

"Good." Pedro hops down so he can see himself reflected in the window. He waggles his ears. "Now, tell me. What's going on?"

Margie takes a deep breath in and blows it out. "My mom signed me, I mean us, up for a mother-daughter quilting class."

I nod my head a few times. I can't fathom it. "I see."

"Do you believe that? Quilting? Mother-daughter?" Margie *ughs* into the phone.

I can't help it; a laugh bursts from my throat. "Sorry. That is just so funny."

"What is? What's funny?"

"Now I know where you get it. All the plotting and arranging things—that's your mother." Another oops. That might not have been the best thing to say. "I'm sorry. You're not like your mother. Except maybe a teeny bit." I shrug my shoulders at Pedro. Too bad he can't talk; maybe he could get me out of the hole I'm digging for myself.

"Just for that, I'm cutting up the Camp Casey tee that you gave me. You can see the scrap of it in my memory quilt."

"Oh, man. That's cruel. I said I was sorry." I'm mostly sure that Margie is kidding, that we're just teasing each other.

"Okay, okay. Maybe I'll keep that shirt." I can hear Margie's mom calling her. "But I'm cutting everything else up into little squares. Everything."

"Fine. Keep the Casey tee though. If you only have one shirt, that's a good one." Pedro waves good night to his reflection and returns to the bedside table. "I know. You've got to go."

"Yeah. I'm afraid, though. What's next? Mother-daughter lion taming?"

I laugh again.

"Shut up, McKane."

"Yeah, yeah. Goodnight." I wave to my reflection in

the window and past it to Margie as she rifles through her clothes in her bedroom, in her house down the street. "Be careful. Lions have claws."

"Roar!" Margie says. She covers the phone. I can tell because there are the loud scrapes of muffled sound. My skin prickles at the rustles. I can barely hear her yell, "I'm coming." It's as though she went far away and then came back, in a quick second. As clear as a bell she says, "Gotta go."

"Okay. See ya tomorrow."

"Yep. Tomorrow." Margie hangs up.

Breathe in and out. My heart races from the jolts of sound at the end of the call. Samantha said I wouldn't always be so easily triggered. I'm glad of that, because right now, every little thing seems to set me off.

I think I'll leave the spiders to build their webs. Go to the living room for a little father-mother-daughter TV. It's safe enough—there's no requirement that I cut all my favorite things into tiny little squares.

Chapter 28

I come in from school, throw my backpack on the chair in the foyer, and limp into the kitchen to hunt for something to eat. Mom and Dad will be in there, cooking, just as they have every other day this week and last. Predictable; I like that.

"Dinner smells great." I open the fridge out of habit more than anything else. "I'm hungry." The leftovers in the yogurt cup make my nose wrinkle. I have no idea what it is. "I watched Margie, Matthew, and Sean run laps today. I really worked up an appetite." No one laughs. I'm not sure they get that I'm making a joke.

"Perfect timing. Dinner is almost ready." Mom moves from here to there, in and out, from the kitchen to the dining room. "You two take your seats. I'll be right in."

"Can I help?" I offer and Mom says no. That's the way it's been every night.

"No. Nope. I've got it," she says. She moves quickly from place to place.

"You had a workout, eh?" Dad rubs his belly on his way to the table. He's preparing to be happy and satisfied.

He and I take our seats. Since she came home, Mom's been setting the dining room table with linen napkins and our good silverware; we've been eating together, family-style. I'm starting to get re-used to it. It's nice.

"How was school?" Mom places the casserole dish on the table in front of my father. "Careful. It's hot."

"Mmm, macaroni and cheese." I grin from ear to ear. If I had thought of it, mac and cheese might have been my favorite meal.

"With hotdogs," Mom says.

Dad is all teeth and smiles, too.

"So, how was school?" Mom asks, again, as she takes her seat.

"It was good." I scoop large spoonfuls of dinner onto my plate. "We learned about Jung and the meaning of dreams."

"Oh, my." Mom wipes her mouth with her napkin. "That's advanced."

"If you have any dreams you want interpreted, I'm your girl."

Mom hesitates, freezes, then coughs. She takes a few gulps of water and turns to stare at the darkening window.

"You've made another great dinner!" Dad pipes in, taking a serving of macaroni.

"You sure have. This is delicious." It is good. Mom does know how to cook.

"I have a dream." Dad sits back in his chair. "I keep

dreaming that I'm down at the track with your mom, and we're watching you run and run." He slaps his stomach. "What do you think that means?"

"It means you're nuts."

There's a pause, a beat, a moment. I reach for my glass and almost knock it over in the process. I'm a dolt.

"You two. You're birds of a feather. Always teasing." Mom dabs her mouth again with her napkin. Her hand trembles.

"Which reminds me. I got us a 'Monday night' present." Dad runs into the other room, and returns with a poorly wrapped clunky thing. It's fairly tall, with bumps and gaps in the paper, and a bow stuck to the side. He sets it in front of me.

"What's this?" I ask.

"I told you. It's a Monday present." Dad takes his seat. "Open it."

Mom leans forward in her chair, but clutches the arms as though she's afraid she's going to fall.

"Me?" I look from Dad to Mom and back. "Maybe Mom should open it."

"She'll get to enjoy it. Though this gift is especially for you." Dad rubs his hands together. He beams. There's no mistaking, he's pleased as punch.

I pull at the wrapping paper and it comes apart, revealing a 12-perch, deluxe bird feeder. "Wow, this is great, Dad." I get up and give him a hug. "Thank you." He is a smart, smart man.

"Richard, that's wonderful. Just wonderful." Mom stands, brings a shaky hand to her throat. "I think, since we're celebrating, we should have a toast."

She goes into the kitchen. I hear her humming, opening drawers and cabinets. She returns with an open bottle of white wine and three glasses. She pours some in a glass for Dad and some in a glass for me.

"Mom, I don't want any." I squeak when I say this. My throat tightens.

"Oh, of course." Mom cups my face with her hand, tilts my chin. "You're so beautiful, so grown up; I forgot that you're just 14." She finishes filling my glass then picks it up and returns to her seat. She carries the glass in one hand and the bottle in the other. I swear she teeters like an old wino. But I don't think she's been drinking; it's the medication that makes her wobble.

"I propose a toast," Mom says, holding up her wine glass. "You can just use water." She points to my water glass, and her bony finger wavers even more. "As I was saying, 'I propose a toast—"

"Mom! Is it okay if you drink that?" I look at Dad, at Mom; they both appear clueless.

"Andrea," Dad says, "it's just a glass of wine."

"But is it okay for Mom to have wine?" I twist my napkin around my wrist. "With the medication?" I'm wringing my hands and napkin both.

"Sweetie, you don't need to watch over me like that.

I'm supposed to take care of you, remember." Mom laughs, brushes her throat with her fingertips, and takes a sip of wine.

"I shouldn't have wine either, since I have to go to work in a couple of hours. Why don't we all toast with water?" Dad stands, lifting his water glass. "I propose a toast—"

"Richard, stop." Mom's voice lowers, gets heavier. "It doesn't set a good example to have a child dictating to her parents what they can or cannot do." Mom places her wine glass on the table. Her eyes fade to gray.

"Come on now, everyone settle down. We were having a nice dinner. Let's just relax." Dad uses his 911-emergency voice—it's smooth like a just-pressed shirt. "Weren't you baking earlier?" Dad lowers his chin toward the table like a dog sniffing for food. "Do I smell pie?"

"After dinner, you can have pie. Not before." Mom purses her lips at Dad, shakes her head. Her expression flickers between laughing and sneering.

"Right you are. Dinner first." Dad resumes eating. Mom and I follow his lead. We are quiet except for the clicks of our forks. I keep my eye on Mom. She appears to keep her eye on me.

The food tastes sticky and cold, no longer good. Mom doesn't drink her wine, but she turns the glass by squeezing the stem between her fingers. She pushes at her lips with her tongue. I lose my appetite.

I stand to clear the table, "Oh, I forgot to tell you guys—Margie and I are going to study tonight. We have a test this week—on Jung." I pick up Dad's plate, and Mom's, too. My hands quiver like Mom's; I almost drop her fork on the floor. "I'm going over there. I'll be back around 10." Dad leaves for work at 8:00. Hopefully, if I'm not home, Mom will go straight to bed after he leaves. It isn't that she's done anything crazy; I just don't like tonight.

"You're going to her house?" Dad rubs his hand over his head. "And you'll be back by 10?"

I nod. Dad scratches the back of his neck. I rarely go to Margie's to study; more accurately, I never go there, period. She always comes here so she can get a break from being with her mom. I don't know what's so tough about it—I like her mom. But if she wants to study here, that's always been fine with me.

Dad nods like he gets that something is up, but that he understands as well. "Okay, but be back by 10—no later."

"Thanks, Dad." I'm moving at the speed of light, faster than a speeding bullet. I can't wait to leave. Mom twirls her glass and watches me, then turns to her reflection, sharpening in the blackened window. She's silent except for an occasional clucking sound.

I grab my jacket, backpack, and head out the door. "Bye. Back by 10." I leave without giving Mom or Dad a chance to respond.

I don't care that no one is home at Margie's. Tonight is the quilting class. Margie made a big deal about not wanting to go. In truth, I think she likes the cutting and sewing and combinations of color and texture. This is the first time since Mom came home that I had to get out of the house. I just had to; I was dying inside. At least there's space and oxygen and room to breathe out here in the wide night air. Samantha said there might be nights like this, when I just want more room.

I'm cold, shivering actually, and it's approaching 10. My head tells me to go, but my feet stay planted on Margie's stoop. I remind them that we lied to Dad about studying with Margie; we don't want to lie about when we'll be home, too. My toes begin to wiggle, my legs extend. They don't run, they don't stride; in fact, they forget that I can walk with my air cast. Instead, they proceed with the speed of a one-footed hop. This is how I make my way home.

I enter quietly. Dad will have gone to work, and I'm hopeful that Mom has gone to bed. The front of the house is dark—that's a good sign.

"Mom?" I whisper. No response. Another good sign.

I hang up my coat and leave my backpack in the foyer

chair. I tiptoe to my bedroom, no easy task in the walking boot.

I flip on the light. My bedroom swirls like a kaleidoscope being turned. I hold up my arm in front of my eyes as though I'm blocking the sun.

"Mom?" Squinting, blinking, looking through the blur of water, I see my mother sitting on my bed. My eyes understand what my mind does not yet comprehend.

First I see the wine bottle on the floor, empty. Shit! My eyes dart to the left and right. I'm trying to make sense of what I see. There's trash everywhere. The floor is littered with pillow stuffing.

"You've never liked me, have you?" My mother's words are slow and thick.

"Mom—you should go to bed. You look tired." My words are scared. Mom has my box in her hand. She's holding the picture of the two of us.

"That's my box," I say without thinking.

Mom picks up a paring knife from the bed.

"You are so much like your father. He also tells me to go to bed, although for different reasons." She draws lines on the surface of my bed, slicing deeper with each pass.

"Stop. That's enough." I take a step forward, then back. "Really. We should both get some sleep."

Mom gets up and walks toward me. My knees waver. Her eyes are stormy—gray and thrashing. I retreat another step.

"Do you see this picture?" She holds the photo up, inches from my face.

"Mom, please, I'll show you the box and stuff tomorrow." I take another step back. I near the wall. "I've been studying all night. I'm tired."

"I thought you had courage. That's what one of your medals says." Mom's hair sticks up in certain spots. Her lips pull away from her teeth. She's a snarling dog.

"Tell me who's in this picture." She shoves the photo close to my nose. Instinctively my head pulls back.

"You and me."

"Who else?" She snarls through drool and teeth.

"No one." My back is tight against the wall.

"Who else?" She sneers from the back of her throat.

"No one." I scan the picture, which is difficult to do, as I am cross-eyed looking at it up so close.

"Pedro?" I'm so confused. Pedro is bathing with us in the pool. As a child, I never went anywhere without him. He stayed clean because of all his baths and hot summer swims.

"You loved Pedro more than anyone else, didn't you?" Her question is a challenge. She presses the photo to my nose, then crunches it in her fist. Mom stands in front of me, edging closer. I want to climb down from the wall just an inch or two.

"I was little." The room is spinning faster and faster. I look on my bedside table; Pedro isn't there. "Where is he?" My voice rises.

"You'd like to know, wouldn't you?" Mom returns to the bed, tears the photo of the two of us and Pedro into three pieces, and tosses them into my box, smashing the lid shut.

"Mom!" I want to look for him, but my eyes don't trust my mother enough to leave her. "Tell me where Pedro is!"

She has the knife in her hand. She points the blade to the floor. "Poor bastard," she says. "He was sick and needed surgery." Closing in on me again, she holds the knife up to my face. "He didn't make it. We did everything we could." Mom laughs. She laughs and laughs.

"What do you mean?" I can't see Pedro, where my mother points, for all the fluff covering the floor—*for all the fluff covering the floor*.

My mother jabs the knife at the mess. "Poor Pedro." Her voice is singsong.

My hands come up in a rush and knock my mother to the side. "Get away!" I scream.

I fall to the floor. White cotton and gray fur and eyes and ears and stuffing clouds are scattered across the floor. As quickly as I can, I pull together these pieces as though I am racing back in time trying to get to the moment before—before everything came undone.

"Pedro, Pedro," is all I can say through the run of tears that wet my chin, my nose, and covers my face. "Somebody, help me!" I sob as I gather the pieces of him together and settle him on the bed.

"Oh, so sad. Andrea is so sad." Mom creeps up next to me.

She's so close; I can feel and smell the wine-soaked metal of her breath as it presses on my neck.

"Get out of here." I can't breathe, not one, nor two, nor three. I can't breathe. "I swear. You'd better go." The room swirls and I look through the blur of deep water.

Mom raises her hand to me, the one with the knife. I grab it. "Get out!" I yell while holding her in my grip. She pulls her wrist, but I won't let go.

"You aren't well. I know you didn't mean to do this. If you'd just gone to bed."

"Let go," Mom says. She sounds a little frantic. She moves in close so we make a kissing image, butterfly wings, of each other.

"I should have killed you in that pool. Drowned you and Pedro both." She is ugly—her face rubbery and hard. The knife shines between us.

"Mom—" I pull her closer so we are face-to-face, "I wish you had." Instinctively we both stiffen our backs. She turns her face away. And I move forward an inch or two more.

I spit. I spit on her, hitting her cheek. She stumbles backward as though I'd shot her, pierced her heart. Her falling leaves me space to run, and run I do.

Out of the room, out of the house, down the street, past the trees, past the school, past the market, Dino's, the rink. I run and run and run. I forget that I'm wearing a boot or that I ever broke my leg. Pain spreads beyond my leg to my chest, my arms, my back, neck, and head. I am fire in motion. I run like I can run forever, like I will. I run, and run, and run. Past Samantha's beige office with the square tiled rug, past the river, and past a tall row of pines. I run and run and run.

I do not hear *shh, shh, shh*, not once, not ever.

Chapter 29

I run, and stumble, and lurch forward. Exhaustion has overtaken me; I'm running on empty. I stumble, and lurch, and run. Lurch, run, and stumble. I don't know how much longer or farther I can go before I will not be able to take another step, before I collapse like a pile of dirty laundry, unable to get up without help. Lurch, stumble, run.

"Andrea! Andrea! Stop!" My name sails over black air. Vigorously, I shake my head. Don't stop. Look at the road ahead, the ground, the star-pierced sky. Run!

"No!" I croak to the chasing words. "Leave me alone." This is a lot to say on very few in-breaths. Each syllable is expressed through an exhaled burst of steam. "I'm running—"

"Andrea! Wait!" The voice is behind me, gaining on me. I can't keep up. The trees slow their movement. "Andrea!"

"I'm running for help." I stumble, drop to my knees. The dark circle begins to close, encroaching from the outside. Before the black completely overtakes me—I see my father.

"Dad?" I'm enveloped in warmth.

"Yeah, kiddo." He cradles my head, rocks me back and forth. "You're okay."

"Pedro's gone." I let go in painful sobs. "He's dead," I say to my father's heart, where I rest my head.

Dad lifts me up, as though I were a five-year-old, and carries me toward the car. "Matthew," he calls, "get the blanket."

"Matthew?" I'm confused.

"He drove so I could look for you." Dad wraps me in a deep wool blanket. I realize I've been cold for a very long time.

I can't feel either of my legs. "My leg." I can't feel anything. "Help."

"It's okay. Everything's okay." He bends his head over mine, creating a cave for me to hide in. "You're safe."

"I was getting help." Numbness mixes with pain in tight spirals.

"I know. I know." Dad's breath warms my forehead. "And you did."

Matthew opens the back door of Dad's hundred-year-old car. I'm so happy to see it. Dad manages, I'm not sure how, to get us both inside without banging my leg or throwing out his back. I can't stop crying. Dad rocks me back and forth, back and forth. "Shh, shh, shh," he says. "Shh, shh, shh."

I'm shivering, then shaking. Dad closes the blanket around me. Matthew drives.

Margie is the first to spot me when Dad carries me into the ER. She doesn't say anything when she approaches; she just puts her hand on my shoulder. That makes me cry even more.

"McKane," Margie uses her shirt-sleeve to wipe tears off my chin and her own, "you're messing up my makeup."

"No sir. You look great." And she does.

The ER nurse gets me a gurney. Dad has to go to the front desk while I'm wheeled into a room.

"Can you go with her?" Dad asks Margie.

"Sure, Mr. McKane." Margie motions to her mother, standing at the edge of the waiting area, that she's going with me.

I reach for a tissue on the table near my bed. "I can't stop crying."

Margie grabs a couple more for me. "What happened? Your dad called, wanted to know if you were still at my house." Margie continues to hand me tissues as I use each one up. "Were you at my house?"

"Yeah, I sat on your steps for a couple of hours." The acrid smell of medicine reminds me of the last time I was in the hospital, and of my mother's breath. I feel queasy in my head and stomach.

"Your dad called you, something about scaring away the nightmares, and when you weren't home," Margie hands me more tissues, "he called me." She winces like she's hearing a bad sound. "He kind of freaked out—well, for your dad—when I told him I'd been out all evening."

I cringe, too, for my dad, and for the pain in my body. "I bet he did." I grab Margie's arm. "My leg—" I suck in a gasp of air to halt the pain. My shaking worsens.

Margie sticks her head out into the hallway. "Mr. McKane? Nurse? Someone! Andrea needs help." She checks on me, looks out in the hall, then back at me. Now she's freaking out, trying to be out in the hallway, and here next to me, both at the same time.

The doctor hurries in.

"Let's see, what do we have here?" He removes my walking boot and cuts the leg of my jeans—my favorite jeans. He turns my leg left and right. "Keep breathing, Miss—" He pauses. I know he's waiting for me to tell him my name, but my mind isn't forming many words right now. Pain is all I want to say.

"Andrea. Andrea McKane," Margie offers.

"Ah, nice name." He uses a flashlight to look at my eyes. His mouth hangs open. "Looks good. You're doing fine."

"I'm going to throw up," I gurgle.

"No problem." The doctor takes a plastic bowl out of a cabinet and hands it to me. There are so many bowls in the cabinet, it looks like they expect everyone who comes to the ER to heave. "How about you tell me what happened?"

I'm too busy puking into the bowl.

"She had to run," Margie says, "on her broken leg."

"I see."

I'm throwing up, freezing, sweating, throwing up. "There's something wrong," I say.

"I'm getting your dad." Margie returns with Dad in tow.

"Hey, kiddo. Hanging in there?" Dad puts his hand on the top of my head. The boiling of my muscles reduces to a simmer.

Dad extends his hand to the doctor. "Richard McKane."

"I'm Dr. Flaherty." The doctor is the only one who doesn't look scared right now. He's unfazed by my shaking and vomiting. He lifts my leg, prompting more nausea. "As I understand it, your daughter ran with her walking cast on. Is that correct?"

Dad looks at me. I nod.

"That's right. She had to; she had to run on her leg," Margie says.

"Well, we need to take some X-rays and give her something for the pain, which also will help her with the shock. However, I think she may need surgery—right away."

Even though I'm lying on the bed, still I collapse. "Dad? Surgery?"

He pushes the hair back on my head, the way he pretends to do with his own. "It's okay. Everything is okay."

"Where's Mom?"

"She's back at the hospital, the other hospital. She's

okay, too." He squeezes my hand. "What do we need to do?" he asks the doctor.

"I'll send a technician in and she'll take Andrea to X-ray. We'll talk after we look at the films." Dr. Flaherty fills a syringe with medication he pulled from a locked cabinet. "In the meantime, this should calm the shaking and alleviate your pain." He gives me the shot. I turn into melting cheese.

Even my tongue relaxes. "Dad? Will Mom come home again? You know the laws that say she gets to come home, and if she starts doing better and they say she is well enough to come home, and she wants to, does she get to?"

"Easy, kiddo, easy. Wow, that's a fast-acting drug they gave you." Dad takes my hand in both of his. He puts his elbows on the bed and brings my hand to his cheek. "You don't have to worry about Mom."

He returns my hand to the bed, covering it with his. "We'll talk more about it later, when you aren't so loopy."

"She'll be okay?" I close my eyes and rest in a soft cloud that holds me, cradles me. It takes away the lingering pain.

"As well as she can be."

Right here, right now, with Dad taking care of me, I'm home—and as well as I can be.

Chapter 30

Dad helped me dig the hole. I've got a hard cast on my leg after the surgery, and I'm of course back on crutches. The doctors say I'll be like new eventually, and able to run and run and run. Six weeks, eight weeks, isn't that long in the grand scheme of things.

I finish applying mascara and pinching my cheeks the way Margie taught me. The butterfly necklace she gave me looks great against the black silk shirt I'm wearing with my blue jeans. I swear there is a magical power in this butterfly. When I touch it, a warm, calm sensation runs from the top of my head to the tips of my toes.

"Hey, kiddo, Margie's here." Dad is holding up well, considering. He's had to take time off from work to be with me in the hospital and take care of me at home, although Margie and her mom have helped. Plus, he's been going through the process of divorcing my mom. He loves her still, he says, but he wants sole custody of me. He wants me to be the one to choose whether or not I visit Mom or she visits me. This has all been difficult for him, I can tell. He didn't expect things to be like this. Neither did I. It's impossible to predict the way life will go, or where we'll end up when we start running down the path.

"Hey, Andrea—" Margie knocks on the bathroom door. "I hope it's okay but I brought some friends along."

"What?" With a whoosh I open the door.

Margie is standing there with Sean and Matthew behind her.

"Uh—" I grab Margie's arm and pull her into the bathroom. "Excuse us for a second, guys," I say through the crack of the door before I close it.

"You invited Sean and Matthew?" I restate the obvious in a high-pitched whisper.

"Relax, McKane, they're cool. They wanted to come."

"Oh yeah, easy for you to say, you aren't burying your stuffed animal." I seesaw back and forth on my crutches. Even though you aren't supposed to lean on them, I do at times.

"Andrea, I'm serious. They are really okay. Sean brought flowers —for the grave."

"He did?"

Margie nods, brushes my hair back. "So let's go. You look great."

With clunky one-footed hops and steps, we exit the bathroom.

"Hi. Sorry about that—" I shrug my shoulders. "Girl stuff."

Sean hands me a bouquet of yellow freesia. They

smell like green, and sun, and dark earth. "Here, these are for Pedro," he says.

"Thanks." Freesias are my favorite flower, but I don't remember telling Sean that. Both Sean and Matthew are wearing ties. They, too, smell fresh and look sharp.

"I guess it's time." I hand the flowers to Margie and ask her to carry the box, my memory box, with all the mementos removed, and Pedro inside. I added a medallion to the box, one for Pedro. It has the word *Loyal* etched across the front and *Friend* on the back.

I lead the procession out the back door. Dad follows us, carrying a box of tissues. We gather around the hole in the ground. It's under my window, under the bird feeder, under the tree.

A chickadee and several sparrows scatter as we approach. They fly to the next tree, and the next, their bellies full.

Sean holds my crutches for me as I figure out a way to get down to my good knee; I end up having to sit—so that I can put Pedro into the ground. I stroke the top of the box, wanting to leave the imprint of my hand for Pedro to watch. As soon as I rest the box in the bottom of the dark hole, in the soft, rich, dusk-smelling earth, tears run down my cheeks, beside my nose and over my chin.

Dad offers me a tissue, and Margie one, too. Sean and Matthew aren't crying, but that's only because they're trying not to. I can tell.

Sean helps me up. I take a deep breath in, and a deep breath out. Gripping my crutches so I don't quiver too much, I begin, "I love you, Pedro." That's all I can say for several breaths. "I am so sorry." That's it. No more words. My heart hurts. Sean puts his hand on my back. Margie does, too. Matthew puts his hand on Margie's back, and Dad wraps invisible arms around all of us. We stand quietly for a few minutes.

"Matthew, could you hand me the shovel?" I point to the trunk of the tree.

Matthew gets it, gives it to me, and I begin pushing dirt back into the hole. It's awkward as I balance on my crutches, but I'm determined to do it. I place the first two shovels of dirt into the hole, then hand the shovel to Margie; she does the same and hands the shovel to Matthew, who passes it to Sean. Sean hands the shovel to my dad, taking the tissues in exchange. I see tears rolling down Dad's cheeks as he scatters the last shovelful of earth. I place the freesias on the grave. "I'm still going to talk to him. He gave me such good advice."

Everyone laughs.

"Can I still talk to him, too?" Margie asks.

"Sure. But I don't think he can take you to the prom anymore."

"That's okay," Margie wraps Matthew's arm over her shoulder. "I've got a date."

My red, tearful eyes widen and my eyebrows rise at the news. "Pedro's happy about that."

"Sweet dreams, Pedro. Sweet dreams," I say.

There's one more thing I have to do. I take the wishing stone from my pocket, the one Dad gave me, and hold it between my two palms, pressing my wish into it forever and always. Then I turn around, which isn't easy, and toss the stone over my shoulder. Turning back, and seeing Sean, Margie, Matthew, and Dad standing over the grave of my sweet Pedro, I know that my wish has already come true.

Dad leads the procession back inside. Sean puts his arm across my back to escort me. Once again, we have to deal with the awkwardness of crutches that prevent us from holding hands and being close, even when taking a simple walk. Margie and Matthew follow, arm in arm.

"Dinner is served," Dad calls. He's wearing his apron and rubbing his belly, smiling a smile he hasn't smiled in years.

Even though I'm sad, I smile back.

EPILOGUE

"So, Andrea, how are you doing?"

"I'm good, maybe a little nervous. The doc is going to okay me for full-speed running, soon."

"That's wonderful." Samantha is sitting back, relaxed, in her chair. She looks peaceful.

"Yeah, except what if I'm already going as fast as I can go?"

"What if?" Samantha asks, her eyes brightening.

"You're right. It doesn't matter." I rub at the place on my leg where my cast used to be. "Being able to run, that's the most important thing."

"How do you calm yourself when you feel nervous?" Samantha leans forward.

"Well, I need to remember to breathe. Breathing is so important." Samantha and I both laugh.

"That's good. Anything else?"

"I've got my keychain medallions." I hold up my house key and the three medals—*Freedom, Courageous,* and *Strong*—that have been drilled to hang from the ring.

Samantha nods. "Very good. I'm pleased that you take such good care of yourself."

"Me, too." I pass my thumb over each medal, absorbing the impression of the word.

"How about your dream? Are you still having the same one?" Samantha rests her elbows on her knees, puts her fingers together.

I look at my square on the rug, then back at Samantha. "Yes, but it's changing."

Samantha waits.

"I used to run into the water and up toward the girl, but she would disappear, and this black film would close over me before I reached her." I shift in my seat, wanting to get comfortable. "Lately, I run toward the girl, and even though I'm underwater, I hear the *shh, shh, shh* sound of running. The girl disappears and I break through the surface of the water." I swallow, take a deep breath. "That's when I wake up." I tug at the corner of the pillow I hold in my lap. "The thing is, I break through. I do. And I'm not as scared as I used to be."

Samantha waits, she listens, and she encourages me on.

"It's like that when I run. I think I'm going to die, that I'll never make it, and then something happens and I'm flying—I have wings." I hold my arms out like a runner crossing the finish line.

"I see."

But, unlike a runner at the end of a race, I don't stumble and collapse, exhausted, in a heap. I keep on going; I talk to Samantha about Sean, Margie, Dad, and even a little bit about Mom.

Before I leave, I take a square of folded yellow paper out of my bag and hand it to Samantha. "Here," I say.

"What's this?"

"Open it."

She unfolds the paper and reads what I have written: *Thank you! Love, Andrea*

Samantha looks at me and I at her. I give her a Pedro nod. She answers with a smile.

Then I stand, take a couple of steps to the door, open it, and step outside. Sean, Margie, and Matthew are picking me up today. I have no idea where we're going or what we're doing, but I can hardly wait.

ACKNOWLEDGMENTS

First I want to recognize the communities of writers into which I've been welcomed: The Whidbey Writer's Workshop MFA Program, The Good Eggs Critique Group, Sondra Kornblatt's Writing Group, The Creepy Writers Critique Group, and Pesha Gertler's Women's Writing Circle, where it all started. Without the encouragement of these gifted writers, I would not have had the courage to write. I'm grateful to Stephanie Stuve-Bodeen for inviting Whidbey Writers Workshop faculty and students to join her in the dream of writing 50,000 words during National Novel Writing Month (NANOWRIMO). *Running for My Life* is the result of that November frenzy.

Regina Brooks, Jill Goodman, Evelyn Fazio, and Alex Lucci have helped make *Running for My Life* a better book, and helped me to be a better author. I am grateful to them for their insight, honesty, and willingness to share their knowledge and expertise.

Gift from Within, powered by the love and compassion of Joyce Boaz and Frank Ochberg, M.D., has created a safe space for PTSD sufferers to meet and support each other as they seek freedom from their traumatic pasts. The members of GFW have done much for many.

Erika Berry, her father John, and her student Jenna Holmes, offered me invaluable support and feedback on *Running for My Life*. Erika's father inspired the goofy and loving Mr. McKane. Thank you, Erika, for sharing your dad with me.

Even though they've both passed away, my mother, Janeann Smith, and my father, Arky Gonzalez, live in all of my works. I'm grateful to them for loving to write and paint, and for passing on to me their passion for words and art. I hope my work honors their talents. My mother suffered from schizophrenia and was anguished, most of all, by the pain she caused others. My heart goes out to all who suffer from debilitating mental illnesses and to those who love them.

My friends always know the right things to say when I can't find the right words to write. For more than 25 years, Treacy Colbert, Margy Backus, Katie Gallagher, Joan Kwiatkowski, and Marie Esposito have sustained me with words of love and encouragement. Many others have also supported me as I've pursued my dream of writing. Here are some of the many: Martha, Maureen Gonzalez, and the Carroll, Bracy and Nuckols clans, with their gracious and accepting hearts; Chris, Mel, Jan, and Joanie and their families of friends; the Japanese Women's Posse, which made me an honorary member; the family of St. John United; the people I've worked with from Boston to Madison, and from LA to Seattle; Rebecca Bradshaw, and the gracious sanghas at the Seattle Insight Meditation Society, the Cloud Mountain Retreat Center, and my Kalyana Mitta group; Robbie Sherman, M.D., Linda Mihalov, M.D., Nancy Mercer, N.D., Johanna Hoeller, D.C., and Sonia Wang, O.M.D., the all-star team of medical practitioners; and all the other communities that have made me laugh and cry, and challenged me to live fully, with integrity, and connected to all. We are many hearts beating as one.

And last, but greatest, in this long list is Kathy. I love you.